THE ALIBI

VM LARSSON

THE ALIBI

LARSSON MEDIA

THE ALIBI: THE FRILAND MURDERS BOOK 1

Copyright © 2025 VM Larsson

This is a work of fiction. Names, characters, places, and incidents are the products of the author's imagination or are used fictitiously, and any resemblance to actual persons, living or dead, business establishments, events, or locales is entirely coincidental. All rights reserved. No part of this book may be reproduced in any form or by any electronic or mechanical means, including information storage and retrieval systems, without written permission from the author, except for the use of brief quotations in a book review.

ISBN: 978-91-989200-0-0
Cover: The Cover Collection

vmlarsson.com

The Friland Islands are a fictional group of Swedish islands in the North Sea, originating from early Norse settlements southwest of Norway. The Friland Islands consist of 288 islands; only six are inhabited: Friland, Fossa, Breda, Vidare, Holm, and Lunna.

The old Norse dialect known as Frilandic is spoken, and the location is at 57.108233 latitude and 4.789287 longitude. For a detailed map of the Friland Islands and their exact location, head to vmlarsson.com.

List of characters
Moa Bakke – Forensic Technician and a **main character**.
Fredrik Dal – Forensic Technician and a **main character**.

Erik Storm – Forensic Technician and Moa's colleague.
Rasmus Iversen – Detective Inspector.
Ylva Moore – Detective Inspector and colleague of Rasmus.
Anna Vall – Prosecutor and works closely with the police team.
Jan Hager – Chief Forensic Pathologist, owns a hotel.
Ingrid – Is married to Jan.
Hanna – Works at the hotel. | **Tim Klein** – Works at the hotel.
Bernd Jung – Wildlife Researcher, hotel guest.
Stephan Ziegler – Colleague of Bernd, hotel guest.
Lars Gaard – Famous chef, and a hotel guest.
Casper Brix – Carpenter.
Preben Hesselund – Professor and witness.

Henning Hager – Municipal Manager and father of Jan.
Max – A troubled kid. | **Frida** – A trusted hairdresser.

NORTH SEA

A helicopter descends over the wind farm off the island of Friland, its rotors slicing through the silence.

Two men descend; one is alive, and the other is dead.

The relentless thud of the blades echoes in the night as a crescent moon casts a pale glow over the sea. The men are oblivious to the October night's chill and humidity.

Swiftly and efficiently, the team completes its mission. The helicopter banks to the right and vanishes into the darkness.

CHAPTER ONE
Sunday, October 22

The air-sea rescue in Toft on the Friland Islands received an early morning phone call shortly before half past three. A guard on Platform Three had heard a helicopter hovering nearby. Through binoculars, he observed that wind turbine twenty-two, undergoing repairs and stationary, had a body secured to one of its rotor blades.

Simultaneously, the traffic control center raised the alarm. A Maersk rescue helicopter in the area had deviated from its designated route. The pilot was unresponsive to calls, and it rapidly descended.

* * *

Shortly after five on Sunday morning, forensic technician Moa Bakke boarded the search and rescue helicopter with her colleagues, forensic technician Erik Storm and chief forensic pathologist Jan Hager. As the seatbelt tightened, a hunger pang reminded Moa of her sleepless night. Being on call meant light sleep, irregular meals, and constantly being ready for the phone to ring. But that call also brought a familiar thrill and a sense of purpose. The victims depended on her.

Erik sat quietly, staring out the window. His sunburned face now bore a weary, grayish pallor. The marks of sleepless nights were etched beneath his eyes. Beside him, Jan looked like a first-class businessman waiting for his breakfast tray.

Gusts of wind seized the helicopter, causing it to tilt. Moa braced herself, watching as large water droplets splattered against the windows. A police diver's deep voice crackled through the radio.

"The body appears covered with feathers and is secured with lashing straps around the rotor blade. We found nothing at the bottom and are ready to depart."

The helicopter's searchlight sliced through the darkness, illuminating rows of wind turbines resembling solemn gravestones. Despite the grim mission ahead, a surprising sense of peace settled over the brief journey.

Erik sat in silence, his hand gripping one of the handles tightly, knuckles whitening with the intensity of his hold. Moa's private phone vibrated in her pocket with a message. And as usual, the number was hidden.

B.A.U

An object resembling a tumor clung to the far end of one of the turbine's white blades. Moa was determined to prove her proficiency as a forensic technician. Though young, she knew from the moment she collected her badge that respect had to be earned the hard way.

She adjusted her body camera and slipped a small camera into her pocket. The helicopter circled the area and descended slowly. When the door opened, dense, salt-laden night air rushed into the cabin. Moa stepped forward and disappeared into the darkness toward the turbine.

The closer she got, the more intense the stench of death and sour feathers became. A man of average height, his head turned skyward, was fastened to one of the turbine's rotor blades. The body, naked and covered in white feathers, had eyes wide open as if he had made a final attempt to capture as much life as possible. A dead bird was stuffed into his mouth.

Moa carefully plucked the bird from his mouth and placed it into an evidence bag. Someone had meticulously wrapped the body with blue and red lashing straps, securing them with hooks in pre-made loops around the rotor blade. A sticky note with a barcode was barely visible on one of the metallic buckles. Moa adjusted her camera, trying to focus while swaying on the rope. After five attempts, she finally captured a relatively sharp photo. Her priority was to bring back the body in the best possible condition. Signaling back to the helicopter, Moa instructed the crew to retrieve all the straps and buckles.

Her hands and face felt sticky from the salt water, and her scalp itched under the beanie and wig she longed to remove.

Before retrieving the body, Jan performed a preliminary examination. He returned in less than five minutes, struggling to find balance in the cabin despite being fit.

The rescue crew, carrying a net to wrap around the body, disappeared into the spotlight, their overalls reflecting the helicopter's beam.

Erik seemed to have recovered somewhat; his face had transitioned from grayish to gray-green and back to pale. This was their first helicopter ride to a crime scene, and he had never mentioned any issues with motion sickness. Moa pulled the bag with the bird out of her pocket and showed it to him.

"Good job," Jan said, giving a thumbs up.

"Thanks. It looks like the body was pre-packaged with the lashing straps, ready to be attached to the blade. No visible superficial injuries."

Below, the crew cut the straps, ensuring the body remained intact. A sudden gust of wind caused the helicopter to tilt, prompting Erik to grab one of the handles in the cabin quickly.

The radio crackled with urgency, "Return ASAP; the wind is intensifying, making winching impossible."

* * *

Detective Inspector Ylva Moore and three patrol units waited at the port in Toft. The birdman had set off a frenzy, and Moa guessed it would only intensify with each passing hour. The radios buzzed with calls between different units. The nearest patrol stamped their feet, clearly feeling the biting cold.

"Guys, calm down. It's not even winter yet," Erik chided.

"Crap. Got new shoes, too small, can't fit warm socks in them."

"Welcome to life," Erik replied with a smirk.

Moa quickly briefed Ylva on the morning's events, recording her observations at the site calmly and objectively.

Jan followed with his report, and his monotone voice provided a soothing break from the morning's drama.

"I'm handing over the case to Rasmus," Ylva declared.

"We'll see what we find during the autopsy later today," Jan added. "I get the feeling I've seen him somewhere before. Or maybe he looks like someone. What do you think?"

Due to the sheer quantity of feathers covering the man's face, it wasn't easy to discern his features.

"I've never seen him," Moa stated, turning to Erik and Ylva, who shrugged.

Jan muttered a polite phrase and disappeared. Moa carefully collected feathers from the body.

"Did you also make a note of the bird?" she asked Erik.

"I did. Dead bird, number three. Not much, but it's something."

"We're done here. I'll submit a report and get the ball rolling when we get to the station. This case is unlike anything I've worked on before."

"Agree."

"All right then, Icarus," said one of the Falck team members who had come to retrieve the body. "It's time to go."

* * *

A pale dawn peeked between the houses in Toft as they returned to the police station. Streetlights illuminated the path of weary people heading to work or school.

"A sandwich and a coffee from Rikko's since we're passing by?" Erik suggested, stopping at a red light.

"Great idea."

The warmth in the van slowly brought Moa down from the adrenaline rush. Erik hadn't said more than necessary since they left the wind turbine. Despite his role as the forensic coordinator and many years of service, she wondered if he doubted her competence. His lack of enthusiasm was palpable.

As Moa returned to the van with their order, the scattered clouds spread across the sky, and the wind picked up again, adding a chill to the morning.

"Rasmus called," Erik stated. "We need to head up to Nordby. The victim is a missing German who stayed at Jan's hotel, confirming that Jan was right in recognizing him. We'll take his belongings from the room, and hopefully, we can gather some evidence. Maybe the man had visitors."

"Okay, good. We should be ready to leave by nine."

The saltwater had started to make Moa's face itch. Annoyed, she rechecked her phone, which remained silent.

CHAPTER TWO

A sliver of morning light pierced through a thick curtain in a sparsely furnished apartment. Ziggy rose and moved toward the window, stopping just short. The eternal gray rat race loomed outside, among endless rows of identical red brick houses. The worst season was nearing, promising nothing but more drudgery. This lifestyle sucked. He deserved better. A lot of money was at stake, and he couldn't afford to lose focus. He had one week to prove his worth.

Ziggy returned to the desk, his eyes flicking to the news feed on the screen, primarily cluttered with ads for vacations and luxury cars.

Money could buy you anything. And everyone was more than willing to sell their soul. Cheap.

CHAPTER THREE

Through the reception window of The Pier Crown Hotel in Nordby, Fredrik spotted two police cars pulling into the parking lot. His heart rate spiked automatically. Instinctively, he felt ready to step in as a police officer and forensic technician.

Was someone dead in their room?

Had there been a break-in?

He glanced down at his stained pants. A motion-sick three-year-old on the plane had vomited, and the mother had handed Fredrik a couple of wet wipes and an apology. The wipes had only transformed the mess into a large, lemon-scented, stiff patch. These were his only pair because he had mistakenly thrown away his new ones and packed the old ones covered in wall paint.

A woman, who seemed on the verge of tears, set a tray of glossy pastries beside the whole-grain bread and rice cakes. Despite having had an early breakfast, Fredrik couldn't resist helping himself to the food. The woman attempted to smile, giving the impression that she wanted to apologize.

Meanwhile, outside the window, stormy winds raged across the sea. Foamy crests crashed against the sand fences on the beach, greedily dragging sand and seashells into the depths, only to spit them back up with the next wave.

So far, the Friland Islands had embraced him with a sense of calm. Despite the pain in his shoulder keeping him awake for much of the night, he felt rested for the first time. A faint scent of freshly ground coffee wafted through the room, mixing with an undertone of incense and wood.

* * *

A door slammed shut, and two uniformed police officers—a short woman with blonde hair and a taller, bald man with a deep suntan—entered the breakfast area, accompanied by a plain-clothes man.

"Fredrik?" asked the man, stepping forward and extending a hand. In the other, he held a thick folder with bits of paper sticking out.

"Rasmus? What are you doing here?"

Fredrik knew this wasn't a courtesy visit. Rasmus turned to the officers and said, "Fredrik Dal is a forensic technician with the Stockholm Police."

Rasmus turned back and continued, "This is Forensic Technician Moa Bakke and Forensic Technician Erik Storm at the Toft Police."

He gestured toward the couple. Moa smiled and extended her hand; her handshake was firm, but her eyes were weary.

"He speaks Frilandic and German," Rasmus said.

Moa's smile deepened, revealing a hint of a dimple on one cheek. Erik followed with a solid handshake.

"We've met before," Moa replied, turning to Rasmus. "Let's get started with the room."

"You can eat later," Rasmus said, taking Fredrik's plate. "I need a German interpreter. Your timing is perfect. A German man, Bernd Jung, was found dead this morning. He was one of the hotel guests, and I will speak to his colleague who is staying here. I also want your help communicating with the other German guests; I think there are four of them. Do you have your interpreter badge with you?"

Reluctantly, Fredrik glanced at his untouched plate on the buffet table. He pulled out his badge and asked, "What are you doing here? Last time we met, you were working in a fancy office in Oslo with an insurance firm."

"The quiet lifestyle didn't suit me, so I returned to the islands. And you? In a spa hotel in Friland during the low season? Are you sick?"

Rasmus headed toward the reception, with Fredrik following close behind.

"I'm managing a summer cottage in the area."

That was all he needed to say. It sounded good and wouldn't prompt further questions. Rasmus continued to the office behind the reception. The weeping woman was talking on the phone.

Rasmus flipped through his folder and said, "The last time Stephan saw Bernd was Friday afternoon. When he didn't show up for dinner, his colleague got worried. Bernd's wife called several times during the evening without getting an answer."

Rasmus's face bore signs of either too little sleep or too much beer—possibly both. The young woman hung up the phone.

"Jan is on his way," she said, glancing curiously at Fredrik as a middle-aged woman entered the office.

"Fredrik is a forensic technician and interpreter; we know each other," Rasmus explained. "He'll help me interpret when I interview the German guests."

"I'm Hanna," the middle-aged woman said with an efficient, authoritative tone. "I'm the secretary, and I handle a bit of everything. Ingrid runs the hotel with Jan."

"I need your help," Rasmus said. "Is there somewhere we can sit?"

"The conference room. It's adjacent to the treatment rooms. Should I start informing the guests right away? They must have noticed something is going on."

Hanna took charge of the situation while Ingrid, looking helpless, fiddled with her phone. Rasmus straightened up.

"Thanks, I appreciate it."

"What happened to the man?" Ingrid snapped.

"What's Stephan Ziegler's room number?"

"Jan will tell me later anyway. Room one hundred two. The guest list is over there."

Rasmus grabbed the list and motioned for Fredrik to follow him up the stairs.

"Bernd was found at sea, tied to one of the rotor blades of a wind turbine that was stationary for repairs. They must have lowered the body using a helicopter. It was naked, covered in feathers, and he had a dead bird stuffed into his mouth."

A surge of adrenaline shot through Fredrik's veins. He missed his job.

"How was it attached to the blade?"

"With lashing straps, like those used on sailboats. It must have been well-planned. Moa and Erik went to the scene in a helicopter. SAR had their boat in the area, and the Coast Guard is now patrolling the coast with an aircraft. A rescue helicopter from Maersk deviated from its route around the same time and seems to have landed on southern Vidare Island. We have several patrols heading there. The Navy has also deployed a boat. It's starting to look like a circus on the islands right now. How long are you staying?"

"A week. I have some loose ends to tie up, and I planned to relax and read a couple of books."

Rasmus laughed, struggling to take the final step of the stairs.

"We'll have a beer later when things calm down."

Moa emerged from the partially open door adjacent to Fredrik's room. He preferred the idea of sharing a beer with her instead of Rasmus.

"Beer sounds good," he said, making a mental note of how easy it was to tell a lie.

Rasmus was the type who was always the last to leave the bar. Occasionally, he sent messages, and Fredrik felt guilty for not keeping in touch. Their conversations usually ended with the promise to meet for a beer again—things people say to be polite but never really mean, though maybe there was a glimmer of hope for reliving a past night out.

Fredrik looked forward to being helpful. Money was always welcome, and he valued the feeling of being needed, especially after almost eight months of sick leave. Returning to work as a forensic technician or detective inspector seemed unlikely, but this was good enough for now.

CHAPTER FOUR

Moa placed the technician's bag on the floor in Bo's room.

"A tidy man," Erik remarked as he entered the bathroom. "All his stuff is neatly arranged in a toiletry bag."

"It feels like someone else has been here packing up his things," Moa observed.

"Or maybe he did?"

"Why would he do that?" she questioned, sensing Erik was at a loss—unlike him. "Let's go through the room and get this over with," she said. "Grab a paper and pen."

She wasn't comfortable with the reversed roles. There was no time for sluggish colleagues, and she had learned not to ask too many questions. Asking too much risked people, including colleagues, unloading their problems on her, and she already had enough on her plate.

15

"Can you check the bathroom and see what's there and if anything appears missing? Also, look for fingerprints. We must rule out if anyone else has been in his room."

Her sharp voice snapped Erik back to attention.

The new protective coverall she changed into was even warmer than the previous one, and the elastic band of her face mask chafed behind one ear. Rarely did she curse her choice of profession, but this was one of those moments.

Crouching on the floor, she lifted the bedspread and searched under the bed with a flashlight. Apart from a few dust bunnies, there was nothing unusual—a common sight in most hotels. Lavish extravagance, but even the finest establishments could be hit or miss with cleaning. She systematically went through the nightstands, their drawers, and the minibar, letting her gaze sweep across the walls, ceiling, and window.

Why was Fredrik at the hotel? Moa couldn't recall their last conversation—perhaps it was a Christmas greeting? She had thought about him occasionally, wondering how things might have turned out if they had met at the right time and lived closer.

The sound of Erik rummaging in the bathroom snapped Moa back to reality—she was here to work, not to daydream.

"How's it going?" she asked.

"Toothbrush, toothpaste, electric razor, blood pressure medication, eyeglass wipes, and Ocuvite vitamins."

"Nothing missing?"

"Nooo…"

He sounded unsure. What the *hell* was wrong with him?

"I don't think Bernd was the type to use styling products or skin cream," Erik added.

Moa opened the closet, finding only ten empty hangers.

Erik emerged from the bathroom with the toiletry bag. He looked puzzled as if he was wondering: How did I end up here?

"Will you document the contents while I go through the suitcase?" Moa asked.

"How long has he been here?"

Erik placed the toiletry bag in an evidence bag and wrote the date, time, and location on the label.

"According to Rasmus, Bernd checked in on Thursday and was supposed to go home today. Three nights."

Moa spread the contents of the suitcase on the bed. It took less than a minute.

"Note down: one pair of pants, two shirts, a pair of socks, three pairs of underwear, a T-shirt, a keychain, a charger for an iPhone, a laptop charger—what appears to be a Dell—and a book."

"Bernd probably put his phone in his pocket, took the laptop under his arm, and left the hotel sometime after three in the afternoon. What do you think?" Erik speculated.

"It seems to fit. Someone may have arranged to meet him. So far, it doesn't seem like anyone has seen him. Rental car?"

"In that case, Rasmus will contact us, and we'll bring it to the station for a closer look. Given the missing laptop, Bernd might have met someone or sat down to do some work. It wasn't a spontaneous walk."

"Okay, let's pack things up," Moa ordered.

* * *

Eriks phone rang as Moa was about to tell him she was ready to leave. It was almost midday. Maybe she could persuade him to stay and grab a bite before returning to the station. She took a moment to observe the reception area, absorbing the tranquility and longing for a less stressful life. A woman sat sipping coffee in one of the armchairs by the window, her reflection mirrored in the glass. Moa envied her, imagining herself relaxing and enjoying coffee in a comfortable chair. Until then, she had to believe that the new job and the house would be her salvation. After all, when everything was already in dire straits, there shouldn't be any more nasty surprises left.

Moa opened a new message from an unknown number. She knew exactly who it was.

Hi, sweetheart, heard you've moved. Looks like a nice house. Should I come over, or what do you prefer? It's business as usual.

She stared at the message, desperate to pee, hungry and sweaty. The message was from Flemming Smede-gaard—a scumbag and owner of the cosmetics chain Paul & Pia—her biggest mistake.

CHAPTER FIVE

Twenty-five minutes had passed since the police disturbed Fredrik's holiday bliss, and the image of Bernd Jung became clear. Bernd was a dedicated researcher uncovering how migratory birds and bats were adversely affected by wind turbines. His work had ruffled feathers, particularly with three large wind farms surrounding the Friland Islands, with more developments planned. Bernd tried to halt the expansion through lectures and by joining various action groups.

His colleague, Stephan, a man in his fifties, struggled to contain his emotions. Overwhelmed by the news, he needed time to process it. Scheduled to leave the island in the afternoon, he requested to return later for the interview, hoping the initial shock would have worn off by then.

The storm continued to rage outside while a fire crackled in the lobby fireplace. Fredrik followed Rasmus into the conference room, awaiting more information about Bernd. With only a handful of guests at the hotel, it was difficult to go unnoticed. With some luck, someone might have spoken to Bernd or seen something. Even the smallest detail could be the breakthrough they needed.

When Fredrik searched for hotels in Nordby, his options were limited: the luxurious and overpriced Hotel Linden Oasis or The Pier Crown Hotel, which ran a trial opening during the winter. The Pier Crown's cheap deal included the noisy annex extension work carried out next door, but a hearty breakfast buffet with complimentary coffee and snacks throughout the day served as bribes to keep guests' content and complaints at bay.

A whiteboard in the conference room bore a striking message from the previous day's meeting: "We're putting Nordby on the world map." The municipalities clearly had grand ambitions. With the shocking murder, the area was about to be inundated by major news channels, thrusting the entire island into the global spotlight within twenty-four hours.

Guests came and went, but none could provide any clues. As the tension peaked, an elegant man strode in with a tray.

"Time for a coffee break," he announced with a winning smile.

Rasmus didn't even look up from his pile of papers, scratching a peeling rash on his wrist.

Fredrik realized he hadn't eaten since breakfast; it was almost half past twelve. Having coffee and Friland pastries on an empty stomach would only make him nauseous. Rasmus poured himself a cup, took a few sips, scratched his wrist again, and pulled out a blank paper as the man said, "Lars Gaard says he doesn't know anything, hasn't seen anything, and will remain in his room. I think this place is starting to resemble a daycare center."

The man reached out a hand to Fredrik.

"I'm Jan Hager, chief forensic pathologist and owner of the hotel. I heard you're a forensic technician, one of us.

Fredrik stood up and shook hands with Jan while his phone whistled for the hundredth time that morning. Jan gave the impression of having returned from a sunny vacation. With a chiseled jaw and a row of even white teeth, he could easily star in a medical drama, appearing much younger than his actual age.

"Fredrik Dal, that's correct. I'm a forensic technician with the Stockholm Police and an interpreter. I'm here on vacation."

Fredrik glanced at Jan and Ingrid, searching for familial resemblances.

"I'm done here. I'll go talk to the staff," Rasmus said, pulling a nail clipper out of his pocket and beginning to trim his already short nails over a waste-paper basket—an odd habit he had exhibited at the conference in Oslo as well.

"I heard there's a K-9 unit out. Hopefully, the dogs will find something," Jan said, inspecting his well-maintained nails. His rough, raspy voice filled the room.

"Yep."

"Are there many patrol units out?" Jan asked, his gaze sharp and curious.

"Yep. Who is on the night shift at the reception? Other staff?"

"Tim Klein handles the reception. He was off on Friday, so I covered his shift. And there's Violeta, our only cleaning staff, and her husband, the maintenance man. They work irregular hours and might have seen or heard something. Check the schedule with Ingrid."

Jan's phone rang with David Bowie's "Space Oddity," and he declined the call.

Rasmus folded the nail clipper and snapped it into his pocket, looking puzzled at Fredrik as if he was wondering why he was still standing there. A couple of pastry flakes clung to one corner of his mouth.

"And don't forget the construction workers next door," Jan added. "They're in and out of here. I'll ask their boss for a complete list of names."

Rasmus thanked him and turned to Fredrik. "I'll talk to Stephan again around half past two; it would be good if you could be here."

"Okay. I'll grab some lunch now."

"Check with Moa and Erik; they should be done by now. Maybe you can join them?"

As Fredrik walked by, Jan smiled, exuding authority. His black shirt and shining shoes starkly contrasted with Rasmus's entire appearance. Unconsciously, Fredrik's brain registered everything he saw: Oxford shoes, size forty-seven, a matching belt, and a Ralph Lauren shirt.

Moa and Erik were busy loading Bernd's belongings into their van.

"We're leaving now," she said, grabbing the last bag. "Besides, we've been up since the early hours. Have you eaten?"

She wiped her sweaty forehead with the back of her hand.

"I was about to find a place to eat," he replied, feeling a rare surge of hope.

"Join us. We have an hour's drive back to the station in Toft and need to eat. Café Lykken, straight up, first right. Do you have a car?"

"Of course."

"Great. See you there in fifteen minutes."

Fredrik noticed a flicker of joy in Moa's eyes before the door closed behind her, and she was gone.

CHAPTER SIX

Moa found solace in the warmth of the restroom at Café Lykken. She lingered for a while, letting the warm water flow over her hands. Chilled to the bone from the morning at sea, she still felt the remnants of sweat from the hotel. The lemon-fresh scent of the soap tempted her to rewash her hands, allowing the stress and turmoil to fade away momentarily. Reluctantly, she returned to the table, grateful it wasn't summer and peak season; only a few tables were occupied.

Erik ended a call, placing his phone face down on the table.

"It was Rasmus," he said. "He wants as much information as possible about those buckles."

"We'll do our best," Moa replied. "Given the number of stores around here that might sell lashing straps for sailboats, there should be a few, especially since we're close to one of Friland's largest ports."

"You did well out there," Erik said.

She sensed the compliment didn't come easily to him. Erik tucked his phone into his pocket and stood up.

"Thanks."

He gestured toward the restrooms while scrutinizing his hands. He hesitated momentarily as if he wanted to say something, swallowed, glanced around the bright room, and ran a hand over his forehead.

"I've started having issues with heights."

Moa nodded.

If he didn't overcome his fear of heights, it could create problems at work.

Fredrik approached the entrance door, and a brief, intense shockwave surged through Moa's stomach when his eyes met hers.

CHAPTER SEVEN

The café's maritime theme, with its white-painted pine paneling and large white lanterns scattered on the stone floor, made Fredrik long for summer.

"Why didn't you tell me you were coming?" Moa asked.

"I had no idea you were here on the main island," Fredrik replied.

Erik approached, smiling as he shook off the excess moisture from his hands.

"I've never washed my hands for so long," he said

Fredrik knew the feeling all too well. Even with gloves, the specter of death seemed to seep through the protective layers. As the shift neared its end, the presence of evil lingered like an ominous halo.

"That was the strangest crime scene I've ever been to," Moa said. "And we traveled by helicopter. I have to admit, the wind farm is beautiful from above. It was a majestic experience. I hope to fly over it again someday, preferably on a sunny day. And off duty."

"The police divers came up empty-handed," Erik added. "But I guess we can't expect to find a knife full of fingerprints waiting for us on the seabed."

"I heard from Rasmus that the man had a bird stuffed in his mouth," Fredrik stated.

Moa shook her head, pressing her fingertips against her temples, and said, "When you think you've seen it all. Let's hope it leads us somewhere."

"Any visible injuries on the body?"

Fredrik pictured the scene, almost feeling the sea breeze in the night air.

"No. The man showed signs of asphyxia with bleeding in the eyes. I suspect it was pre-packed to be attached to the rotor blade via helicopter. It was the most physically demanding crime scene I've ever investigated."

"Your Frilandic is impressive," Erik noted, glancing at Fredrik.

"I studied Frilandic dialect and Old Norse extensively, as well as German, Icelandic, and English. Languages have always fascinated me."

An elegant woman approached the table and started chatting with Moa. It was clear they knew each other. Fredrik caught snippets of the conversation: "Closing soon for the winter," "Canary Islands," "golf," followed by a muffled laugh before she took their order.

Fredrik's phone vibrated in his pocket, reminding him he should have contacted his wife, Irene. He had sent her a text informing her of his arrival, thinking it would suffice for now.

Hunger pangs began interfering with his concentration, and he was glad he had ordered a large steak. Erik placed a napkin on his lap while Moa examined the heavy forged cutlery with black handles, almost as if she was considering slipping them into her handbag.

"It's likely more than one perpetrator," Erik stated. "If someone has access to a helicopter, we're talking about people with money and resources who know how to play their cards."

"Unfortunately, he's right," Moa agreed. "We need to focus on our part of the investigation and gather evidence. There has been a lot of controversy around the wind farm, with many environmental activists wanting to prevent more from being built. Ideally, they would like to shut down the existing ones, if possible."

Moa rested her chin in one hand, gazing into the room. Fredrik tried not to stare at her. Her shoulder-length blonde hair needed combing, and freckles adorned the bridge of her nose. He wouldn't mind looking into her light blue eyes first thing in the morning.

Before Fredrik could ask the next question, she continued, "FONG Energy owns the wind farm Vidare One, where Bernd was found. In addition to Vidare Two, they are already building a third. Green Air, a new company, plans to enter the market and build the North Park wind farm nearby."

"There are rumors they're negotiating to put up another one about twenty kilometers near the neighboring island," Erik added.

"In addition to the competition, experts say there will be more impact on the wildlife," Moa said. "There are news reports about it every week. So far, they have a long way to go before they get permission. But I doubt they'll get it. Besides, building a new hotel close to the sea in Nordby has been approved. The municipality is, of course, happy about it and wants to attract more tourists."

"Everything and everyone can be bought for money," Fredrik remarked.

"You're probably right, unfortunately," Moa agreed.

Their lunch was served, and Fredrik realized he hadn't eaten properly in two days. His lunch at Arlanda airport got mixed up, and being short on time, he ate it, but the sushi was more like a snack than a proper meal.

The meat on his plate was covered with unhealthy butter, a delicious creamy mushroom sauce, and accompanied by a generous portion of seasoned fried potatoes.

The pale October sun eventually succumbed to the rain, and the asphalt outside Café Lykken darkened with moisture.

"Environmental activists wouldn't kill one of their own, would they?" Fredrik wondered.

Erik replied, "It's illogical unless they want it to look like someone else did it."

"On the other hand, no logical crimes exist," Moa stated. "Both Ylva and Rasmus will have their hands full if they're going to interview everyone at FONG and the platform staff."

"Are there many platforms?" Fredrik realized he wasn't up to date on the number of platforms and wind farms in the North Sea—or any others, for that matter.

"Only one," Moa replied. "Poseidon is the service platform for the employees, so they don't need to commute by boat or helicopter daily. For safety reasons, FONG Energy recently built a smaller platform because Vidare One is relatively close to the shore. Activists and vandals started to appear, so Platform Three was built with 24/7 staffing by at least two people. It was the security guard at the platform who raised the alarm."

"There are several gas and oil platforms further out in the North Sea," Erik added. "We can't rule out that the helicopter he heard passed through the area."

"FONG Energy—it sounds Chinese," Fredrik said. Moa smiled.

"Friland Oil and Natural Gas, FONG. Fortunately, this area has always been relatively quiet, spared from severe crime. Our local constables mainly handle break-ins and minor incidents at summer cottages. The future of Toft's old station had been up for discussion for a long time. Eventually, they sorted it out by building a new station, thanks to Jan, who helped fund it. We also got a new forensic station with a lab for research and education."

"Jan is the king of the hills here in Friland," Erik added, wiping his mouth thoroughly with the napkin. "He's involved in just about everything. It probably helps that his dad is the municipal manager. They're both very driven, and their businesses create many new jobs."

"Is Jan the father of Ingrid?" Fredrik asked, immediately regretting his naïve curiosity.

"They're a couple. Jan recently turned fifty; she's, I believe, twenty-eight," Moa said, scraping up the remnants of the sauce with the last piece of potato. "They met in Switzerland when Jan worked as a company physician and Ingrid as a receptionist at a hotel. It sounds fancy, doesn't it? He has a business mind, and I believe he built the hotel for her. They plan to attract quality tourists from Japan to the islands."

Moa smiled with a hint of sarcasm in her expression.

"Well, they sure know how to keep themselves busy," Erik said. "They've promised to create more job opportunities by expanding."

"Hopefully, our islands will remain quiet, especially in the tourist areas. How are things in Stockholm?"

"About the same as in most major cities, unfortunately. Organized crime is the new normal, and there are a lot of weapons circulating throughout the country. Drugs are reaching even the youngest. Gangs have begun targeting the homes of family members, and everyone feels at risk. And explosives have replaced fistfights."

"Since I moved back to my old neighborhood in Odde, outside Toft, I can manage work-related stress in a completely different way," Moa said. "Closing the door, listening to the silence, and knowing the patio furniture is still there in the morning is nice. It's those little things that make life more enjoyable."

Fredrik perked up. She mentioned *she* had moved.

"I'll call you later tonight, around eight o'clock," Moa whispered. "By the way, are you here alone?"

He nodded. The word alone had never felt so liberating as it did at that moment.

"Is everything okay?" Her eyes searched his face with curiosity.

"I've been shot. I'm on sick leave."

CHAPTER EIGHT

FUCK THE POLICE was scrawled on the wall beside a grocery store sign boasting they stayed open until nine in the evening, even on Sundays. After a quick round, Fredrik found what he was searching for. Without hesitation, he planned to remove the pricey wine from the minibar and replace it with cheese, cold cuts, and potato salad.

He walked through the reception toward the makeshift interview room, where a stillness had enveloped the hotel, reminiscent of the calm after a storm. Only three rental cars remained in the parking lot. A few hours ago, it had been packed with police cars.

Rasmus sat in the same chair. The odor from his leather jacket forced Fredrik to take shorter breaths. As he pulled out a chair, Bernd's colleague, Stephan, arrived. His eyes were swollen, and his hand trembled as he held a piece of paper.

"I need to leave in an hour," he announced. "I've been thinking a lot." He placed the paper on the table, sat down, and said, "Here's a list of the groups and organizations he was active in. Several are open groups on Facebook. He was also a moderator on a few forums. He stepped back because the increased hate and comments weren't leading to anything constructive. Ultimately, the politicians always have the final say in everything."

Fredrik jotted down notes while translating for Rasmus, who was about to ask something when Stephan continued, "Before we left, Bernd said, 'They won't be pleased' when we discussed the new findings about migratory birds. He was supposed to present the news at yesterday's lecture."

"Do you have any idea who 'they' were?" Rasmus asked.

"Anyone who doesn't understand the value of nature. Capitalists."

Fredrik assumed politicians also fell into the capitalist category. The list of potential suspects grew longer by the hour.

"Threats are part of everyday life if you care about the environment," Stephan said. "It's nothing new. Bernd even received threats from his people at one point. A small, newly formed group thought he was spending too much time on his research in Friland and should focus on issues in Germany instead. The problem is that birds migrating north pass directly through this area."

Stephan pulled a pair of glasses from his shirt pocket. "As I mentioned, I've listed the groups, forums, and organizations Bernd was active in. Unfortunately, I can't offer much more help. We mostly talked about work."

Rasmus's jacket squeaked as he moved, and a gray curtain of rain replaced the morning light streaming through the windows.

"Who was supposed to attend the lecture?" Rasmus asked.

"A few researchers from the Netherlands and Germany, and a handful of students from Vidare Island. Some stay at the big hotel by the campsite, and others in cottages. Professor Preben Hesselund organized the lecture."

Stephan got up, ready to leave, but hesitated.

"Oh, I almost forgot," he said. "Major Tom. I can't recall if Bernd mentioned him or if I saw the name in his notes. It stuck with me. As far as I know, Bernd didn't know any military personnel. But if I remember anything else, I'll get in touch as promised."

He glanced at his watch, emphasizing his need to leave. Fredrik and Rasmus thanked him and followed him outside. Fredrik reminded himself that he wasn't involved in the case, wasn't on duty, and should go to his room and nap. Yet, the need for justice wouldn't allow him to relax. How could anyone even think of attaching a body to the rotor blade of a wind turbine?

"I'll head off," Rasmus said. Maybe we'll have that beer tomorrow night?"

Rasmus didn't wait for an answer. Fredrik took the opportunity to fill his lungs with fresh air.

"By the way, did you get any information from the guy who refused to leave his room?" Fredrik asked.

"Lars Gaard? Don't you know who he is?" Rasmus laughed, appearing relaxed for the first time all day.

"Should I?"

"Right now, he's Friland's most famous and hated chef from the TV show 'Our Food.' He recently exposed one of Toft's most exclusive restaurants, Polaris, for using fake Parmesan cheese, ham, and feta cheese. They also claimed to serve Kobe beef. It turned out to be ordinary beef from Argentina. He's not very popular right now."

"What's he doing here?"

"I guess he's taking a break, like you. He said he needed to get away for a while. I'm watching him; he has a bad temper and friends in the wrong places. Not a good combination in a murder investigation."

CHAPTER NINE

Fredrik leaned back in the armchair and stretched his arms, savoring the comfort. A chocolate had been placed on the pillow, and the curtains were drawn, creating a cozy atmosphere. Less than twenty-four hours had passed since he arrived.

He found a small notepad with the hotel's logo on the desk and scribbled down his to-do list: "Monday, call the carpenter Casper Brix and visit the cottage. Morning walks? Buy a pair of pants."

Pulling the armchair closer to the bed, he propped up his legs and added to the note: "Take naps—every day."

Feeling satisfied with his priorities, Fredrik called his wife, Irene. She answered immediately, her voice laced with concern.

"Why didn't you answer when I called?" she whined. "I've been worried."

"I got caught up with the carpenter. He's busy all week and wanted to go through some things with me while he had time," Fredrik explained.

"Did you transfer the money? I have a therapy session tomorrow."

A tight knot formed in the pit of Fredrik's stomach, the familiar grip of stress he constantly tried to escape.

Her therapist charged ninety-five euros per hour. Irene insisted that Fredrik not transfer the payment directly, claiming it was part of the therapy so he could start trusting her again. He hadn't even considered whether he had or if he ever would.

Quickly tallying his account in his head, Fredrik knew there was money, but ninety-five euros for an hour of therapy felt too steep. He had to be careful until his insurance claim was settled.

"I will transfer the money," he said.

A brief silence followed. Fredrik pulled off his socks and wiggled his toes, waiting.

"So, how's the cottage then?" Irene almost whispered.

"It's great—a fantastic little place. I was surprised. It will be fully booked once the summer kicks in."

He didn't believe a word of it. Nothing in life was plain sailing, and no one came to the rescue when shit happened.

"Are you still angry? We can figure this out. The therapist thinks..." Irene's voice trailed off, and he could hear her walking around, fiddling with something and making irritating noises.

"You know, I'm a bit tired. I'm in pain and need to lie down for a while. It was a long day. I'll transfer the money later. It'll be fine."

It won't be fine.

He had already made plans, and Irene was not included, but he wasn't sure of the next step. Maybe he was afraid of venturing into the unknown. He would remember the moment his brain finally said, "Enough is enough."

"I'll be in touch."

Fredrik ended the call, opened the album labeled Family on his phone, and scrolled to a picture of Ronny next to Dennis. His sons were eating ice cream on a sunny summer day. Their last summer together.

A door slammed in the corridor.

Did life have to be so damn complicated all the time?

He felt woefully unprepared for Nordby and the surrounding area. As the new owner of a summer cottage, he should be more informed. He glanced at the stack of tourist brochures he had picked up and began to read. According to the photos, Nordby was a typical summer destination for families. The lighthouse at neighboring Hedborg, which he could see from his window, was known to be located at the westernmost point of Europe. It stood thirty-nine meters high with one hundred seventy steps.

He read about the bunkers the Germans built on the beach during the Battle of the Atlantic, left there as stark reminders of humanity's darker times. A zoo was nearby, and there were many long sandy beaches and numerous festivals to attend. Despite Nordby's small population of only four thousand residents, the area swelled to around ten thousand during peak season.

The idea of taking invigorating walks on the beach every day immediately tempted him. Though he had barely arrived, he felt eager to settle into the cottage. According to his dad, it would be winterized. Nordsol managed the rentals and had only one booking for two weeks in November. He could easily imagine starting a new life here; what was there to return to?

He smiled, relaxed, and fell asleep.

* * *

Tine's call startled him awake. The room was cold and dark, and he longed to hear her soothing voice.

A year ago, they had traveled to Vegavik, a campsite on Fossa Island, north of the main island. They were sent to collect evidence from a cottage rented by a man suspected of murdering two Finnish guests in the sauna at the Scandic Hotel in Stockholm. That's when he met Moa. The day he got shot, he was working alongside Tine, who saved his life.

"Is this a bad time?" she asked.

"Not at all. I'm caught up in the middle of a murder investigation. A German researcher was found dead by a wind turbine. By the way, he stayed here."

"There?"

"In the room next door."

Fredrik rolled onto his side, grabbed a pillow, and placed it under his head. If he closed his eyes, he might fall asleep again. Tine's monotonous voice was soothing, almost like dictating a story.

"Rasmus, whom I've told you about, is working on the case," Fredrik continued, recounting the day's events and how he had acted as an interpreter.

"It's a strange coincidence you ran into two familiar faces in one day. You certainly don't have to go far for some action."

"I've had enough action for now. I plan to relax for the rest of the week."

Laughter echoed outside Fredrik's door, followed by a man speaking German. The voice grew louder, shifting from friendly to commanding. Fredrik pressed his ear against the door, unable to resist, and opened it slightly. A tall, bald man with a broad, muscular back and a bull neck stood farther down the corridor. He recognized him—Tim Klein, the receptionist.

Tim had a crooked nose, likely broken, and three dots tattooed between his thumb and forefinger. Fredrik would instantly categorize him as suspicious based on reasonable and probable grounds. Seeing him behind the reception desk in an impeccably pressed white shirt had made Fredrik temporarily set aside his preconceived notions.

Tim shifted his weight from one leg to another, uttered something rudely, and abruptly ended the conversation.

"Scheisse," he snapped before turning around and walking away.

CHAPTER TEN

Irene's face appeared on the display, but Fredrik declined the call. Lying in bed, he watched the steady twinkling of the lighthouse, focusing on the light until he discerned its pattern: three flashes every twenty seconds.

Moa's ringtone broke the silence.

"What happened?" she asked.

"Everything. And you?"

She laughed. Her ability to find something positive in any chaos would make it easy to love her.

"Pretty much the same. How did you get shot? I assume it was in the line of duty?"

"It happened in a vulnerable area—double homicide in an apartment. The crime scene was secured. We were about to leave. Blood was everywhere, from floor to ceiling. A lunatic with a Glock was sitting by the window in the building across and fired at me. As you can imagine, all hell broke loose. My colleague Tine was behind me. She could have been hit in the head."

"Oh shit."

"She had the presence of mind to get me down on the floor and ensure I was okay. She stopped the bleeding. Strangely, it didn't hurt then. It got worse later. And you?"

"Well, it's been up and down, I suppose. When did this happen?"

"In February. I've been on sick leave since. The bullet fractured part of the collarbone and tore apart ligaments."

Moa's voice softened. "Are you okay now?"

"I'm still on sick leave. Either the injury hasn't healed properly, or I didn't get the correct treatment. I've had two surgeries, developed scar tissue, and dealt with constant inflammation. The rehabilitation plan crashed."

"I'm so sorry."

"Thanks. But it's a matter of continuing and pushing forward," he said.

"What are you doing in Nordby?"

"I'm now the proud owner of a cottage that's being renovated. I was surprised by how quiet and peaceful it is here."

"Autumn and winter are the best times if you're looking for empty beaches and tranquility."

"So, what else is new?"

"I left Glenn and rented a small townhouse near the old harbor in Odde, a short drive from Toft. I wake up every morning to the sound of fishing boats."

There was a moment of silence. Fredrik wished he had also moved somewhere, started over, and ended all the drama associated with a breakup.

"It's on the rocks," he said. "Only a matter of when and how to end it. I'm working on it; it's a long story."

"It usually is. Dinner tomorrow?"

"Absolutely," he said, sensing a glimpse of the lifestyle he envisioned on the horizon.

The beer with Rasmus would have to wait; hopefully, it would fizzle out. Moa asked the question he had been dreading.

"How are the boys?"

"Dennis is studying art in Amsterdam. Ronny... Ronny chose to end his life. That's another long story."

Fredrik heard her gasp, and he could almost feel her pain and compassion. Even when faced with death regularly, fully disconnecting from emotions remained a challenge.

Moa's tone shifted from soft and personal to the efficient, work-oriented voice he was accustomed to as she gave him her address.

"I'm really looking forward to seeing you," he said.

"Same here. We have a lot to talk about."

Fredrik transferred the money to his wife. It would keep her calm for a while. She promised to call after her therapy session the next day. He didn't dare tally up the total cost of all her visits.

Swallowing two painkillers, he curled up on the bed and quickly fell into a deep sleep.

His phone startled him awake. The screen lit up with an unknown number and the country code 0031, the Netherlands. Dennis must have changed his number. It was almost midnight.

"Dad, it's me. I borrowed a phone. I've been robbed."

CHAPTER ELEVEN

Ziggy shivered in his car, the dim streetlight casting a faint glow that made the ice crystals on the windshield sparkle. He craved a long drag of a cigarette despite having quit years ago. His emotional centers were mainly intact, but the urge to smoke grew stronger with each passing hour.

A message on the screen illuminated his face.

There are opportunities here. Great opportunities. And lots of money.

It was true, and he could have written those words himself. But with opportunities came troublemakers. Jealousy, hate, and doubt lingered in the shadows.

His hands were stiff from the cold. Had he slept, or had he merely dreamt of sleeping? Perhaps it was the other way around. Rolling up his sleeve, he injected hope into his vein. Slowly, the blood flowed more freely. His breath formed a mist on the window. The darkness and anguish etched into the night would soon fade. It was time to level up. The game started anew, day after day.

Ziggy rolled back onto the road, grinning as he passed the police station. A new day hovered on the horizon.

He found a packet of gum in his pocket and savored its icy mint flavor. With each bite, his teeth broke into the hard shell, reminding him of his situation and what he had to do: crush the resistance and the opponents.

CHAPTER TWELVE
Monday, October 23

Moa was the focal point of the morning meeting at the forensic department. A bleak dawn painted the classic Nordic palette in grayscale outside the window in Toft.

Hailed as a hero for her work at the turbine, Moa had captured everyone's attention. The "Birdman" case dominated the headlines, and international media flocked to the main island.

"It might be necessary to get assistance from our colleagues in Sweden. We'll start by cutting holidays and bringing back retired personnel. You all know the routine. Moa did an excellent job out there," Erik praised.

Moa almost expected applause. She was no longer the new, inexperienced member of the team.

As soon as the meeting ended, Bernd Jung's autopsy awaited. There wouldn't be enough hours in the day.

"I'll be the lead investigator," stated Rasmus. "Detective Inspector Ylva Moore will assist me. We're working on assembling a team to help us.

"During the day, we'll appoint a suitable crime scene coordinator. Tips are pouring in from the public, and we've established a new hotline for any information related to the case. Be prepared for overtime."

No one had anything to add. The team was accustomed to a strong work ethic. Even the residents of the Friland Islands had teamwork ingrained in their DNA, and everyone was prepared to help during a crisis.

Rasmus continued, "I spoke briefly to Preben Hesselund, a researcher and environmental activist. He was supposed to conduct the lecture Bernd was scheduled to attend. Preben didn't have much to share, mostly reiterating what I already knew. I suspect he's withholding something. The German police contacted Bernd's wife. She mentioned her husband had received threats but didn't believe they were serious. It was mostly nonsense, she said. The German police collected a computer from his residence."

Rasmus glanced at his colleague Ylva, who sat beside him neatly dressed and arranged her reports in a tidy pile.

"Simon Sherman," Rasmus continued, picking up a pen and checking the top line of his notepad. "The security supervisor on Platform Three was alone. Usually, there are two. His colleague called in sick, and they couldn't find a replacement on short notice. I've checked the sick colleague's alibi, and it's confirmed." He crossed out another point.

Ylva had her notes printed, unlike Rasmus, whose handwriting was messy. She had started as a detection dog handler at customs in the port and had moved on to the police.

"Moa and Erik?" Rasmus asked without looking up from his notes.

"All the material has been sent," Moa said. "We expect the fingerprint results from Bernd's hotel room today. I have some things in the lab that need closer examination. We're also waiting for information about the barcode on the buckles from several stores. I'll get someone to assist me with that. They could have been purchased online."

"Or from a store nearby. We hope that's the case," Erik added.

Rasmus continued, "Then there's the helicopter found on Vidare Island. It turns out the helicopter that deviated from its route was a rescue chopper from Maersk. This happened simultaneously as Sherman raised the alarm. The pilot, an experienced Norwegian aviator, Richard Fredriksen, had picked up a seasick engineer from the Tora East gas platform." Rasmus picked up a paper and said, "Elis Fischer, a German engineer, needed urgent hospital care. The pilot changed course and did not respond to calls. After two hours, a plane spotter found the helicopter abandoned on the southwest side of Vidare Island. Traces in the sand indicated three people had dragged something, likely a RIB boat. A smaller pleasure boat, possibly stolen, was drifting outside the wind farm. We haven't tracked down the owner yet. Someone must have waited with the dead body in the boat."

A brief silence followed. Rasmus checked the time, his face showing signs of stress, and turned to the prosecutor, Anna Vall.

"We assume we are looking for three individuals," he stated. "Richard, the pilot, rented an overnight apartment in Toft. When it was searched, it was found empty. Elis Fischer, a German citizen, is registered at his parents' address in Ostritz, a small community on the border with Poland. According to the German police, he has no criminal record, but his name has appeared in investigations: minor drug offenses and forgery. Nothing led to prosecution. Elis is divorced, has two children, and hasn't paid child support for three years. Richard's apartment was meticulously cleaned from any evidence, and traces of alcohol were found," Rasmus detailed.

Rasmus's phone rang, interrupting the meeting. Moa, feeling parched and hoping for a moment to grab some water and perhaps a quick bite, silently prayed for a break.

"It was the Norwegian police," Rasmus announced. "Richard Fredriksen is at home in Drammen with a cast on his leg. They're investigating if his identity might have been stolen. At least we have a name: Elis Fischer, who needs money. I've ensured his cabin is sealed off. We need every bit of evidence. They've secured shoeprints in the sand and on the floor by the helicopter on Vidare Island, along with several fingerprints, a couple of hair strands on the seat, and a piece of chewing gum."

"A new team is on their way to search through it again," Erik added.

Anna cleared her throat, looking like she wanted to say something. "If they continued by rubber boat, is there any chance..."

Rasmus cut in. "I checked departures from Vidare Island airport. A private plane took off at eight and headed for Berlin with four passengers. I'll keep digging to find out more. They could have used different boats or checked into a hotel under false names."

"What about Simon Sherman, the security guard?" Anna asked.

"Twenty-five years in the service, looking forward to retirement. Stable finances. Nothing suspicious," Rasmus replied, flipping a paper. Despite his sprawling handwriting and scattered Post-it notes, he seemed to have everything under control.

"I'm not wasting any time. I'm heading back to Nordby," he said. "I ran into a colleague from the mainland staying at the hotel. He's a forensic technician and interpreter and helped me interview the German guests. I wouldn't be surprised if he saw or heard something. And I'll see if we can find witnesses, checking with business owners in the area for anything unusual. Ylva will check the hotels on Vidare Island, and we need to search the coastline inch by inch. They might not have gone far."

He paused, signaling he was finished.

"Is there any footage from the surveillance cameras at the hotel in Nordby?" Anna asked.

"They haven't been linked up yet," Moa replied. "I hope we can find the RIB boat today, but I don't have much hope, considering how easily they can be transported. Whoever did this must have had significant resources to pull it off. I wonder if they got the wrong person."

Everyone paused, absorbing her words.

"Let's hold onto that theory for now," Rasmus said, giving her an approving nod and ending the meeting.

CHAPTER THIRTEEN

Moa's phone vibrated in her pocket with a message from Flemming. She quickly typed that the money was on the way and prayed he would keep quiet. Flemming had been her next-door neighbor growing up, a highly respected businessman on the island, and a family friend. When her younger brother stole a bottle of cheap perfume from his store, Paul & Pia, Moa had been called out. She was a newly graduated constable, and without thinking clearly, she offered to pay for the perfume. She had waved her Visa card in front of Flemming, who had secretly filmed their conversation. The footage made it look like she was trying to bribe him.

She dared not show the footage to any digital forensics at the station. Her face was mostly turned away from the camera, and the footage had been edited. As a rookie, she had no chance of defending herself in court.

"Police officer bribes business owner" didn't sound good.

Flemming wanted sex in exchange for his silence. Moa managed to negotiate a sum of hush money, but his leverage over her only fueled his relentless pressure. For the first time in her life, she battled an intense urge to kill.

CHAPTER FOURTEEN

A group of Japanese women gathered around the break-fast buffet at The Pier Crown Hotel. Dressed in city clothes, they stood out among the hikers. They looked curiously at the food on the serving trays, laughed, and took selfies. Fredrik smiled politely at them and greeted Ingrid and Hanna as they swept past.

The sound of carpenters starting their shift reminded him that most people had jobs to do, and that life continued despite everything. Dennis's trembling voice had brought forth a new wave of unease; hence, Fredrik had not slept well. Learning that his son had been forced at gunpoint to withdraw cash from an ATM and hand over his phone and watch left him feeling a mix of fear and disgust. Dennis was shaken but unharmed. He had borrowed a phone and some cash from a friend, and Fredrik had transferred the money. With the balance in his account low, Fredrik made up his mind. It was time to act.

Enough is enough, whispered the voice within.

Casper, the carpenter, called with more bad news. They had found another leak in a pipe, forcing them to tear down half the wall in the bedroom.

"Unfortunately, we'll be delayed," he said. "I've set up a fan to dry things out before we can patch it up. It seems to have been leaking for a while; we found mold when we removed the wall panel. The bedroom furniture doesn't smell great. We're working as fast as we can."

"Thanks," Fredrik replied, trying to mask his frustration.

"You can check with Nordsol; they might help you arrange new furniture. You weren't planning on staying here for long, right?"

"A week. I'll have a word with them later."

Fredrik tried not to clench his jaw, letting the conversation with Casper fade. He poured himself another cup of coffee, contemplating his limited options. He wished he could share his troubles with Moa so that he could let the unpleasant events of the past weeks surface. But his logic told him it wouldn't help. Turning back time wasn't an option. Until he owned his life again, he would take small steps forward, one at a time, without looking back.

Instead, he called his dad, the only person who knew the story.

"How's it going? What do you think of the cottage?"

"I haven't been there yet. I'll head over after breakfast. Got involved in a criminal investigation yesterday."

His dad had seen the news and responded with "oh" and "gosh" in the right places.

"Are you at home?"

"I'm waiting for your mom to return."

"Does she know about the money? About Irene?"

"Not in detail. You and I agreed. It will be fine. Relax."

Fredrik looked around; the Japanese women were gathering their belongings. His inner voice told him not to be so damned paranoid.

"I'll buy out the cottage, and we'll be done with this."

"How are you going to manage?" his dad asked.

"I'll find a solution. And I'll be in touch."

Fredrik was about to say thank you when his dad ended the call. Feeling grateful made him uncomfortable, like an irritating itch he couldn't scratch.

His coffee had gone lukewarm and bitter. As he stood up, a sharp twinge in his shoulder reminded him of his limitations. Hanna was clearing tables, assisted by a woman whose bleached hair looked like fried straw. He recognized her from the corridor, pushing a cleaning cart. The Japanese women gathered at the reception, giggling and talking to Ingrid. Fredrik forced a smile, but it felt hollow. Everyone had their polished façade, hiding lurking shadows. He felt shame and anger towards Irene for mismanaging their joint savings account.

How could a happily married man not notice his wife had stopped depositing and was instead withdrawing money?

Why the hell didn't you ever check the account?

Why did he let Irene handle the economy?

If he hadn't been shot, he would have worked evenings, weekends, and nights to catch up. His case was now in a pile of reports on someone's desk. He hadn't received any crime victim compensation yet. The Social Insurance Agency threatened to cut off his allowance by the end of the year unless he accepted a part-time position at an insurance company. They deemed him fit for work.

His shoulder throbbed with persistent pain. The prescribed painkillers were either too weak or too strong, making him nauseous. Having never dealt with severe pain before, he was shocked by the lack of adequate pain relief offered by the healthcare system. Counseling and relaxation exercises only added to his frustration.

Several weeks remained until the next payment was due, and Fredrik urgently needed to find money.

He found his list and checked Casper's name. On impulse, he dialed Irene's therapist's number. The therapist, who had previously worked with the police on debriefings, now saw only a few patients.

He sounded pleased when he recognized Fredrik's voice; he was chatty and liked to befriend the police.

"It's very unfortunate about Irene. As you know, we tried the proven methods, but Irene's choice to end the sessions doesn't mean we failed," he said.

"Things happen. Well, it's been a while. How long now?" Fredrik waited, hoping the therapist would take the bait.

"Exactly. You're right. Seven months, and when she's ready to start over, get in touch. By the way, what did you want? Sorry for talking so much."

"I wanted to check how you are getting along with your plans to buy a boat since I'm considering the same thing."

"Oh, right. I think I've found a Nimbus Nova, so now I must convince my other half."

It was almost ten o'clock. Outside, the sun shone brightly, but inside Fredrik, darkness raged. Nothing would ever be the same again.

* * *

Fredrik arrived at his cottage, nestled in a sunny clearing surrounded by coniferous and deciduous trees with crowns shifting into orange hues. The black wooden house had a partially covered porch adjacent to the entrance.

Had Fredrik been a tourist, he would have turned back immediately. The moment he opened the door, a sharp odor of mold hit him.

The living room had a worn-out red sofa with blue cushions and two mismatched armchairs. The walls and ceilings, covered in lacquered pine paneling, gave the place a dated 1980s feel. Forgotten tools and pieces of wood lay scattered in one corner.

He peeked into the first bedroom, where a bed had been moved to access the damaged wall. Half of the paneling was torn off, and pieces of wood were stacked on the floor, waiting to be nailed up. A fan was running, but the stench of mold began to sting his eyes and make him cough. As he headed back through the living room, a cuckoo clock and a bouquet of faded plastic flowers in a green vase on the coffee table caught his eye.

A quick glance through the patio door at the back revealed more coniferous trees. He felt ashamed, and his self-esteem suffered a blow. Moa was not to see the cottage until it was renovated. His dad had made decent money from the rent and should have put more effort into keeping it tidy. The deal was for Fredrik to manage the rentals until he and Irene sorted out their finances. His dad seemed happy to be rid of it, unaware of its value or potential. The account was in the black for now, but when Casper's work was done, there wouldn't be much left, even if the insurance covered a significant portion.

On his way out, Fredrik spotted a crowbar resting against the wall. He paused, looked at it, and adrenaline started pumping through his veins. Without hesitation, he picked it up with a couple of smaller pieces of wood and a door wedge, placing them in the trunk.

CHAPTER FIFTEEN

If The Vault, the station's staff restaurant, were listed on TripAdvisor, it would easily snag a top rating. In most cases, attempts to create a pleasant working environment in government buildings fell flat, but The Vault was a rare exception. A private company ran it with several successful restaurants across the island; it was so popular that there were jokes about needing reservations.

Moa considered returning for seconds—the freshly made lasagna was that good.

Ylva pushed her empty plate aside and said, "You're back early. Already finished? Where's Erik?"

"He went straight to Richard's apartment to check if anything had been missed, then headed to Tora East to help search the cabin. The autopsy wrapped up sooner than expected."

Ylva looked up from her phone, placing her elbows on the table. She locked eyes with Moa as if she had expected a detailed rundown of the autopsy.

"Three students helped us remove the feathers from the body," Moa began. "As we suspected, Bernd was strangled. No other injuries."

Ylva's phone buzzed incessantly. She glanced at the screen, then back at Moa, and said, "I've been thinking about what you said—about them getting the wrong guy. I'll check with Rasmus about speaking to Preben again. Anna's already been on my case about it."

"Do you think Preben was the intended target?"

"Maybe. Or maybe he knows more than he's letting on. He could be involved."

"There might be something there," Moa agreed. "People rarely live up to our expectations. How did things go at the hotels on Vidare Island? Did you find anything?"

"Unfortunately, no. No recent check-ins that match our information," Ylva said, as her screen lit up with a call from Rasmus.

Moa listened as Ylva responded with a series of monotonous yeses and nos. She glanced at her phone—still silent. It was a relief not to be needed by anyone. Her mind wandered to what she might cook for Fredrik, settling on tossing a couple of ready meals into a pot with some rice. The more she thought about him, the more she allowed herself to indulge in the fairytale she'd created. There was a glimmer of hope, however faint. It was madness, but she couldn't help enjoying it.

Ylva put down her phone. "We've got confirmation that the Norwegian pilot's identity was stolen. Rasmus had a photo of Richard Fredriksen and checked the surveillance footage at the airport. The guy who flew the helicopter looked like Richard."

Moa straightened up, letting go of her fleeting fantasies of a normal life, and asked, "How does Rasmus manage to do all this at once? Wasn't he supposed to head to Nordby?"

"He never gives up. The Norwegian police called right after our meeting. He went straight to the airport to talk to Maersk."

"They must have been pretty embarrassed."

"Definitely," Ylva replied.

"Did he mention the private plane that took off from Vidare Island?"

"Yeah, it was chartered by a brokerage firm. The passengers have been identified, but unfortunately, none match who we're looking for."

"Then we'll have to keep digging."

As Moa stood up, her phone buzzed. She answered the call, following Ylva into the corridor while listening intently to the voice on the other end.

"That was Poseidon Marine Store here in Toft," she informed Ylva. "They confirmed that the barcodes on the buckles match a purchase made in their store on Tuesday. The buyer was a man named Casper Brix."

CHAPTER SIXTEEN

A dog barked on the beach, drawing Fredrik's attention. He turned and glanced toward the lighthouse, where a few figures moved steadily upward, pausing to point out toward the sea.

Curiosity led him down to a bunker on the beach. A narrow opening at the back caught his eye. Inside, the ground was littered with empty cigarette packs, a crumpled square of foil from a condom wrapper, and an abandoned cookie package. Graffiti covered the walls, with "JESUS IS ALIVE" scrawled beneath a gun slit on one side. As he turned to leave, something shiny caught his eye—a USB drive half-buried in the sand. Without hesitation, he used a tissue to pick it up, careful not to touch it directly. On his way out, he stepped into fresh dog poop.

Back at the car, Fredrik noticed clouds blurring the horizon, the serene atmosphere making Nordby feel like the idyllic paradise it was reputed to be. He decided to explore a bit more before finding a clothing shop, so he headed to the zoo. A narrow road that transitioned into a gravel path led him to his destination, where holiday cottages dotted the landscape.

A larger residential building with an adjacent barn marked the entrance to Nordby Zoo. A tall red fence over two meters high enclosed a cluster of white-painted houses. Signs at the entrance read: OPEN 10–18, ADULTS 12 EURO, CHILDREN 6 EURO.

A bus pulled into the parking lot, and Fredrik counted the passengers as they made their way to the entrance— forty adults and five children, racking up over five hundred euros in ticket sales. He moved closer, surveying the facade. He didn't spot any security cameras, which made him smile as he politely held the door open for the last tourist.

Security lock. Five bolts.

Peeking into a large room dominated by an enormous counter, Fredrik cast a quick glance across the ceiling and walls—still no sign of cameras. He stepped back outside, giving the fence one last once-over. It offered perfect protection from prying eyes. The slightly elevated, narrow windows on the left side were visible from the parking lot and the road, yet they, too, lacked cameras. Intrigued by the expensive security door, Fredrik's mind raced with possibilities.

CHAPTER SEVENTEEN

Ziggy took a step forward as if trying to ground himself. The morning's euphoria had long faded, leaving behind a raw, festering wound on his soul. He caught himself craving the rush of killing again—only this time, with more intensity. He knew the risks and could easily delegate the task to others, but it wasn't the same. The hardest part was trusting anyone to do it right.

He glanced down at his hands. They were made for murder.

CHAPTER EIGHTEEN

Back in his room, Fredrik inserted the USB drive into his laptop. A single file popped up—Major Tom.jpg. He opened it to reveal two drawings. One showed a cluster of twenty houses located near the lighthouse and the golf course, with the houses encroaching on sections of the course. The other drawing seemed to depict small islands scattered in the sea. Intrigued, he saved the file and immediately called Moa.

"That sounds interesting," she said after he described what he'd found. "I know Rasmus is in the area today; call him, and he'll collect the drive."

As Fredrik wiped the mud off his pants, a knock on the door startled him. The lock buzzed, and the maid with the yellow hair—Violeta T, according to her name tag—peeked in, looking horrified.

"Oh, I'm so sorry, excuse me," she stammered.

"It's fine. I was on my way out. Could you get a pair of pants washed for me?" Fredrik asked, handing her the soiled trousers.

She placed them in a bag, noting his name and room number. For a moment, Fredrik felt a strange role reversal, as if she were collecting evidence.

"So, you are the cop," Violeta said cautiously.

"That's right, but not on duty. I'm a tourist now," he replied with a smile, noticing a shift in her brown eyes. She hesitantly smiled back.

Fredrik called Rasmus as he headed downstairs.

"Where are you?" Rasmus asked.

"Outside the hotel, about to grab something to eat. Hey, I found something."

Fredrik lowered his voice, glancing around.

"What did you find?"

"Wait a second," Fredrik said, closing the car door. "I found a USB drive in a bunker near the hotel. You should take a look at it. Are you nearby?"

"I'm close. Where are you headed?"

"Café Lykken, I think."

"Are you going there or not?" Rasmus asked, irritation creeping into his voice.

"I'll be there in five minutes," Fredrik assured him.

* * *

Rasmus looked as concerned as he sounded on the phone and immediately ordered a coffee. Fredrik handed him the USB drive.

"What's on it?"

"Only one file with two drawings. Construction is planned near the lighthouse and a few smaller man-made islands. Could this be tied to Bernd's murder?"

"Anything's possible," Rasmus muttered.

"The file name caught my eye—Major Tom. Didn't his colleague mention something about a major?"

Rasmus fiddled with his phone, wiped the greasy screen with his sleeve, and let out a dry chuckle.

"A bit of a stretch, but your imagination is good. Did you save the file?"

"What do you think?"

Rasmus fell silent as the waiter set down their coffees. His eyes darted around the room, barely registering Fredrik's words as he sipped his coffee and checked his phone. The odor of sweat clung to him more noticeably than the day before. He'd changed his T-shirt, but it looked like he'd slept in his clothes.

"Where'd you find the drive?" Rasmus asked, finally focusing.

"In the bunker closest to the lighthouse."

"Simon Sherman from Platform Three confessed he fell asleep during his shift," Rasmus said. "He woke up to a noise, thought he was dreaming, and only realized something was outside when he saw the helicopter disappearing."

"Did the cameras catch anything?"

"We're reviewing the footage now. So far, it backs up his story—looks like he was asleep."

Fredrik hesitated before asking, "What about this company, Green Air? Do they have any ties to FONG Energy?"

"I assume they're competitors, but with so many investors, who knows? And remember, everyone has a price."

Rasmus seemed jittery, his restlessness palpable.

"I need to get back to Toft," he said, heading to the bar to pay the bill. "The coffee's on me. You look like shit; get some sleep," Rasmus added before making a swift exit.

"Thanks," Fredrik murmured.

Rasmus paused at the door and said sharply, "Delete that file. There will be a lot happening here."

CHAPTER NINETEEN

Moa stood outside Hotel City in Toft, eyeing the narrow alley between the buildings and the fire escape at the rear. She liked what she saw.

She returned to her car and pulled out her second phone, the one with the prepaid card. It was time to end the blackmail once and for all. The stress of Flemming's relentless demands had cost her more than money; she had lost all her hair, a constant reminder of how deeply he had gotten under her skin. All she wanted was an everyday life—success at her job, something to look forward to, and maybe a relaxing vacation now and then.

Moa reread the message and hit send.

I'll give in. Book the suite at Hotel City in Toft tonight.

CHAPTER TWENTY

Moa's quaint medieval townhouse on the outskirts of Odde was easy to spot.

"Today would have been perfect for a day off, sitting on the porch with a cup of tea," Moa said as she welcomed Fredrik inside. "Did you have any trouble finding the place?"

He glanced around the small hallway, no larger than a few square meters, taking in the cozy space. A warm, spicy aroma drifted in from the kitchen.

"Not at all," he replied, handing her a bouquet he'd luckily found at a nearby store.

"I can't remember the last time someone brought me flowers. Thank you, that's thoughtful," she said, her expression softening.

He kicked off his shoes and followed her through the living room into the kitchen. The low ceiling, with its white-painted pine paneling, reminded him of how he envisioned his cottage.

She placed the flowers on the table, already set for two, and turned to him with a smile and asked, "So, how was your day?"

"Eventful," he said honestly, watching as she turned off the stove and lifted the lid from a pot.

"It's nice to see you out of uniform for a change."

"We even match," Moa said, nodding to his dark blue chinos and white shirt with blue stripes.

Fredrik accepted a glass of non-alcoholic wine as Moa brought out two elegant glasses. She poured the same for herself.

"Don't let life get in the way of your dreams," he said, feeling a surge of wisdom as he raised his glass to her.

"That sounds like a good motto. Cheers to that, she said, raising her glass. Come on, let me show you upstairs before we eat."

They climbed the steep staircase to a tiny bedroom with a sloping ceiling. The walls and ceiling were made of finely sanded, untreated pine, giving the space a warm, natural feel.

"This is it," Moa said, spreading her hands as if presenting a hidden treasure.

"Can you see the stars from here?" he asked, nodding toward the window, forming a small alcove above the bed.

"I probably could, but I usually fall asleep as soon as my head hits the pillow," she admitted.

"Wow," was all he could manage, feeling a twinge of envy. His shared bedroom with Irene was cluttered with things neither used nor liked. It made him realize that sometimes, you must reach a point of excess to truly appreciate simplicity.

As they descended the stairs, he noticed a golf club hanging upside down on a hook by the front door.

"Do you play?" he asked.

"Occasionally, but it reminds me that I should play more. And if I ever have uninvited guests, it could double as a self-defense tool," she joked. "I've played a few times with Jan in Hedborg; his dad owns the golf course there."

Despite knowing Jan was close to Ingrid and old enough to be Moa's father, Fredrik couldn't help but feel jealous at mentioning his name.

"I should ask about your golf handicap, but since I know nothing about the sport, it probably wouldn't make much sense."

"It doesn't matter. I'm half-decent, and that's good enough," Moa said, setting the food on the table.

"Did you manage to connect with Rasmus?" she asked.

"He came by Café Lykken. He seemed preoccupied, probably focused on the investigation."

"Both he and Ylva are under a lot of pressure. Did you know Rasmus is also a helicopter pilot? I think the military wants him back. With that job, he'd have regular hours. He loves what he does, but working odd hours isn't easy for anyone."

"He never mentioned it. But we haven't had much time to catch up yet."

"He was in the military, then left to train as a police officer," she explained.

"Sounds like he's the perfect guy for this case."

The food was as delicious as it looked—spicy chicken in a rich sauce, served with rice dusted with vibrant yellow turmeric. Fredrik, who considered himself a lousy cook, savored every bite, appreciating the well-prepared meal. For once, he ate slowly, enjoying the flavors before bringing up the maps he found.

He decided not to mention that he had saved the file or Rasmus's advice to delete it. It was easier said than done to stay out of the investigation. But Moa couldn't resist talking about work.

"The last thing discussed at the meeting this morning was the theory that they might have targeted the wrong man when they killed Bernd. Rasmus said he'd keep that in mind."

"How's the prosecutor? Is the team working well together?"

"Anna Vall. She's worked in Norway for a few years and knows Rasmus from before. She and Ylva don't see eye to eye. They're both perfectionists but in different ways. Anna likes to leave no stone unturned, which is good. By the way, they brought in a guy you might have seen today—the carpenter in charge of the extension at your hotel, Casper Brix."

"I might've seen him around."

The pain in Fredrik's shoulder was temporarily dulled. He moved carefully, aware that he needed to be in good shape for what would likely be a long night.

CHAPTER TWENTY-ONE

Fredrik helped Moa set the table, and for a moment, it felt like they had been living together for years. When Moa accidentally spilled sauce on her blouse, they laughed when Fredrik tried to help her wipe away the stain.

Her phone rang. She glanced at the screen in surprise.

"It's Jan," she said, answering the call. Her expression grew distant as she listened, her eyes fixed on a point beyond the room. She ended the call with a simple "Okay," shook her head, and rubbed her temples.

"What happened?" Fredrik asked, sensing something was wrong.

"There was a significant amount of material under Bernd's nails," Moa said, her voice tinged with disbelief. "The lab ran tests in the elimination database and got a match. It matches Rasmus. Jan called to warn me. He's already informed Ylva and Anna, and they've issued an arrest warrant for Rasmus."

Fredrik's mind raced. "But…"

Moa cut him off. "Bernd must have tried to defend himself. But Rasmus? He has connections, sure, but to be involved in a murder? It doesn't add up."

Fredrik knew it was time to come clean. He had saved the file from the USB drive despite Rasmus's instructions to delete it. Now, everything Rasmus had said took on a new light.

"You must tell Ylva tomorrow," Moa urged.

Before anything else happened, he was about to add.

"I'm sure Rasmus has a reasonable explanation."

"If it was Rasmus, he must have had help," Moa speculated. "This isn't something one person could pull off alone. But I still can't see why Rasmus would be involved with something like this. He doesn't strike me as someone with a grudge against migratory birds, and I don't think he knows anyone on the FONG Energy board. What about the carpenter? Maybe he's involved in a bigger construction project—a lot of money could be at stake. Or perhaps Rasmus was being blackmailed. He's always had a lot on his plate and never really relaxed. Ylva mentioned last summer that Rasmus investigated sensitive information linked to the municipality."

"We'll have to wait and see," Fredrik replied, his mind racing. "I'm sure there's a reasonable explanation. One thing usually leads to another, and who knows, maybe he's in debt?"

"I don't think anyone at the station, least of all Ylva, is eager to start investigating Rasmus's private life. Hopefully, they can bring in someone from the outside for that," Moa said, a hint of weariness in her voice.

Fredrik decided to shift the conversation.

"How long have you been living here?" he asked, genuinely curious.

"A little over a year," Moa answered. She continued, reading his thoughts, "They downsized the number of executive positions. Glenn got an offer to work at Europol and moved to the Netherlands, and I wasn't ready to leave the islands."

She sipped her cappuccino, straightened up, and turned to face him. Her eyes were outlined with delicate black eyeliner, and three tiny birthmarks on her left cheek formed a triangle resembling freckles. Moa noticed his gaze on her, smiled, and drained the last of her cup, leaving a bit of foam clinging to her upper lip. He felt an urge to kiss her but held back.

A travel magazine lay open on the couch beside her.

"Planning a vacation?"

"Every day,"

"Where to?"

Moa glanced at the magazine. "The Greek islands are at the top of the list right now. I had planned to go there with my brother, but we never get round to it."

"Does he live near?"

"He was offered a good job at the Faroe Islands, so he's been living there for seven years. But the last time we spoke, he mentioned plans to move back home. And he had done some travel research, so you never know, we might be lounging on a Greek island by the summer."

"Let's go—I'll come with you!"

Moa was quiet for a moment, and Fredrik realized how much he wanted to follow her to the ends of the earth and back. It was a silly fantasy, he knew, but there was something liberating about dreaming. It took the edge off the rat race.

"Deal," she said with a playful smile. "We can start with a day trip to Vidare Island, as tourists this time, and see how well we get along on the road. I'll drive."

Fredrik finished his coffee, liking the sound of that.

"I'll start collecting islands."

She studied him, her tone shifting.

"How are you holding up after everything? Are you okay to talk about it?"

"It's okay," Fredrik began, his voice steady but tinged with sorrow. "Ronny had secured an apprenticeship with a blacksmith for the fall. He was planning to travel through Asia with some friends, you know, that trip you're supposed to take before adult life starts. They'd been talking about it for months—an old Volkswagen van, a few girls joining them. He left a week after he and Dennis celebrated their nineteenth birthday. The plan was for the friends to meet in Vietnam, but Ronny never showed up. A cleaner found him dead in his hotel room."

Fredrik paused, the weight of the memory pressing down on him. No matter how often he recounted the story, it never got easier. If anything, it grew darker.

"I got the news while I was in the hospital. I was shot the same day Ronny ended his life with a cocktail of pills. There were no signs. There was nothing to indicate he was suicidal. The worst part? He had death-cleaned his room. His laptop was wiped clean of personal notes and photos. In his wardrobe, there were a few clothes left."

Moa's eyes filled with tears.

"Oh, dear God," she whispered.

Fredrik reached out and gently stroked her cheek.

"It was like a wake-up call," he said softly. "We lived under the same roof but barely communicated. Neither Irene nor I noticed Ronny was struggling. Life just kept moving forward."

"How did Dennis take it? They were twins, right?"

"It was hard for him. He's managing, but actually not. He called last night—he was robbed."

"In Amsterdam?"

"Yeah," Fredrik replied, his voice tightening. "At gunpoint."

Moa's phone rang, startling them both. She glanced at the screen and showed it to Fredrik—Ylva Moore's name appeared on the display. As Moa took the call, Fredrik's mind wandered back to the days following Ronny's death. The travel insurance didn't cover suicide, so the cost of bringing Ronny home was astronomical. The funeral expenses piled up, and Fredrik had already lent Ronny a significant sum for the trip. He had planned to use their savings, but when he checked the account, it was empty. Irene had drained it to feed her shopping addiction.

When Fredrik confronted her, she broke down and admitted everything. Desperation had led her to take out high-interest loans, and all Fredrik could do, still recovering from his gunshot wound, was to take out a second mortgage to bring back his son's body.

Moa finished her call and turned back to Fredrik, her expression weary.

"Sorry about that. Ylva wants to talk to you tomorrow. Everything is a bit confusing right now."

Fredrik gave her a gentle smile. "I can see you're tired. We can continue talking tomorrow. And let's not forget— we have our little mini-vacation to look forward to."

Moa stood up, wrapped her arms around him, and rested her head on his shoulder. He stroked her back gently.

"You look tired, too," she said softly. "I hope you can sleep."

"I will," Fredrik replied, his tone warm. "After that delicious meal, I'll sleep like a log. You're a great chef."

As he left Moa's home, he couldn't help but admire how well-organized her life seemed. Closing the door behind him, Fredrik mentally prepared himself for the next challenge.

CHAPTER TWENTY-TWO

Moa stepped onto the street. Nothing could go wrong. The cold night air seeped through her clothes and bit her skin as midnight approached. She would have preferred to doze off on the couch with Fredrik after their pleasant meal, but she had other plans.

Her car was parked outside the police station a block away. It was a ten-minute walk to the hotel. A cyclist wobbled by, followed by a taxi. Moa, dressed like any other night jogger in workout clothes with a backpack, blended into the shadows, drawing no attention.

She slipped into the stairwell opposite Hotel City. Despite her steady pace, her heart raced. The metal door to the basement was unlocked, the shiny handle icy against her hand. She flicked on a small torch, its light barely cutting through the darkness. The backpack creaked softly with every step. There was no plan B—no thoughts of what she'd do if someone appeared. It didn't even cross her mind.

In the frigid basement, she stepped out of her sneakers and peeled off her workout pants, revealing thin black fishnet stockings and a short black skirt. She slipped on a pair of natural-colored protective gloves, followed by black mesh gloves. As she changed into a black wig and applied bright red lipstick, the tight knot in her stomach began to unravel. Her breathing steadied. The confident, composed woman who would take control of the rest of her life emerged, pushing the stressed forensic technician aside.

Moa smiled to herself in the darkness, checked her pockets to ensure everything was in place, and prepared for what came next.

Snugly in high-heeled boots with soft rubber soles, her feet moved silently across the cold floor. The urge to flip on the lights and double-check that she hadn't left any trace of her presence was almost overwhelming. But when she heard the front door slam and footsteps nearing the basement door, she quickly swung on her backpack. The elevator chimed before the building fell silent again. Moa crept up the stairs, her heart pounding, and paused to listen. The jingle of keys echoed faintly. Slowly, she cracked the basement door open. The stairwell was shrouded in darkness, offering her the cover she needed to slip out unnoticed.

She turned into a narrow alley between the buildings, glancing up as a faint light flickered in the suite on the third floor. Flemming had sent her a message, saying he was waiting, ending it with a heart emoji. It would be his last.

How many women had climbed this fire escape before her, deciding it would be their last time? She guessed there were many. Each had a dream—to land a good job, start fresh in a new town, sober up, travel, enjoy life, and maybe even find love. But their dreams, never realized, were etched in the invisible shoeprints on the stairs, only to be swept away by time.

A car started in the parking lot, and footsteps echoed on the sidewalk. Even if someone saw her, she wouldn't stand out. She was tempted to grab the railing on the last steps of the staircase but thought better of it. As she reached the top, Moa glanced up and caught her reflection in the back door.

Her reflection stared back at her with haunted eyes, teetering on the edge of regret. Was this a good idea? Was there justice in the world? Would anyone believe her? Karma? Her mind spiraled with doubt, and amid the chaos, a long-forgotten phrase surfaced: "Moa, you're the right person in the wrong place."

Are you sure about this?

For heaven's sake. Pull yourself together.

The deep red carpet in the hallway swallowed the sound of her footsteps.

"I knew you'd give in," Flemming slurred, his breath heavy with the odor of alcohol and anticipation. He grabbed Moa's arm and slammed the door shut. Her backpack thudded against the wall as he lunged at her.

"Easy, boy. We've got time," she said, her voice firm and controlled.

It stopped him in his tracks. His dark blue briefs, too tight, exposed a hairy, sagging belly beneath a white undershirt. Flemming's grip tightened on her forearms, his face mere inches from hers, the veins in his cheeks bulging.

A discreet knock on the door froze Moa in place, her breath catching in her throat.

She heard a childish voice call out

"Flemming? Would you like to play with us?"

He winced and breathed heavily as Moa swiftly moved away from the door. A woman with two light braids, a short skirt, and knee-high socks appeared through the narrow gap. For a moment, she looked like a little girl. She slipped inside, and Flemming's face morphed from surprise to sheer horror as Moa pulled out a handy Taser Stun Gun. Flemming collapsed on the bed, screaming in pain as the girl pressed a pillow against his face. Moa was quick to push a tab of LSD on his tongue and placed a pair of children's panties on the floor near the door. The girl's eyes locked with Moa's, and without a word, Moa pressed a wad of cash into her hand, watching as she slipped out of the room. Flemming lay unconscious, lost in a drugged euphoria, with no hope of recalling what had happened.

Moa swiftly opened the door, retrieved the hidden camera attached to the fire extinguisher in the hallway, stopped the recording, and quietly vanished down the fire escape.

She was going to send Flemming the film revealing how he opened the door to an underage prostitute.

Vilda, a no-nonsense private investigator with a knack for bending the rules, played her part flawlessly. Her services didn't come cheap, but in the end, it would cost Moa far less than what Flemming had been bleeding her for.

CHAPTER TWENTY-THREE

The evening at Moa's left Fredrik feeling relaxed. As he entered the hotel, one of the German guests approached him.

"The researcher, Bernd," the woman began. "We saw him on Thursday evening. He was talking to the man who sometimes works at the reception."

The door swung open, and Tim Klein, the very man she was referring to, walked in.

"I get chills whenever I see him," she admitted. "Bernd was talking to him in the parking lot. It was late, around half-past nine. I was heading to the car to grab something. I got the feeling they knew each other. I didn't think much of it at the time, but it's been nagging me. It would be best to mention it to that police officer you helped. His name was Rasmus, right?"

"Yes, Rasmus," Fredrik confirmed. "Thank you for telling me. I'll inform him and get back to you if he needs more details."

As Fredrik closed the door to his room before midnight, he noticed a series of messages from Irene. They were hastily typed, with misspellings and abbreviations that made little sense.

Standing by the window, he gazed at the distant lighthouse, its steady blink offering a moment of calm. He inhaled deeply, mentally preparing himself for the physically demanding tasks ahead.

All his savings had vanished, his marriage was a sham, and he found himself at a breaking point. It was time to take control and put things right—there were no options.

* * *

At half-past two in the morning, Tim was watching TV in the lobby when Fredrik approached the locked front door. Recent events prompted tighter security.

"Room one hundred four," Fredrik said. "I can't sleep, so I'm going for a drive."

Tim nodded, eyeing him warily. "Okay, I'll let you out. We've got new rules after everything that's happened. The boss doesn't want people coming and going at all hours. How long will you be?"

Fredrik nearly laughed at the absurdity of the situation.

"No more than an hour."

"Room one hundred four? So, you're the police officer from mainland Sweden?"

Tim's tone was probing, his gaze sharp.

Fredrik was already growing tired of his newfound fame but quickly composed himself.

"That's right. I've picked up some mental baggage lately, and the nights are tough."

Tim's expression softened as he unlocked the door.

"Be careful out there," he said. "Wouldn't want you to end up being wanted yourself."

Fredrik couldn't tell if it was a joke or a veiled warning. Stepping outside, he noticed Lars's car was missing from the parking lot. His carefully laid plans suddenly felt precarious. Catching a glimpse of his stress-lined eyes in the rearview mirror, he hesitated briefly.

What the hell am I doing?

The crowbar clanged against something in the trunk as Fredrik drove over a speed bump. He was mentally prepared for what lay ahead. Sooner or later, everyone faces a crossroads where they must decide between right and wrong. He knew what was right but was about to choose the wrong path.

The road narrowed, and the barn and adjacent house were shrouded in darkness as he approached the zoo. He switched off his headlights, relying on memory to guide him. Slowly, he rolled into the parking lot, tucking his car behind a clump of trees. He slipped on a pair of plastic sandals and gardening gloves he had purchased earlier. The sandals were two sizes too big. He pulled a hat over his head and wrapped a scarf around his neck and mouth.

Fredrik rummaged through the trunk, retrieving the crowbar, a door wedge, and three pieces of wood. In his pocket, an empty bag waited to be filled. Without hesitation, he moved toward the entrance behind the fence, feeling for the door handle. It was locked.

He knew it would take at least twenty-five minutes to respond if the alarm were triggered in the off-season—plenty of time. The wooden door frame made the task easier. Taking a deep breath, Fredrik set the wedge and pieces of wood beside him and turned on his phone's flashlight, dimming it to a faint glow. He began chipping away at the door frame with deliberate, precise movements, counting the seconds in his head as he worked.

He wedged the flat, sharp end of the crowbar between the door and the frame, prying it open just enough to slide in the wedge. With a swift motion, he pushed the claw deeper, creating space to insert the pieces of wood. The lock gave way with a satisfying snap, and the door swung open.

Fredrik's muscles tensed with adrenaline; fatigue and pain were distant sensations as he swept the flashlight beam across the room. The counter opposite the entrance beckoned, and an open, empty cash register confirmed they dealt in cash. Sun-faded pictures of animals decorated the walls, giving the place an eerie stillness. Two doors caught his attention—one labeled ENTRANCE and the other STAFF ONLY. He reached for the staff room door handle when the sudden sound of a car engine shattered the silence. His hands trembled uncontrollably, making it impossible to turn off the flashlight. Instead, he pressed the phone against his leg to dim the light.

He crept to the window overlooking the parking lot and watched as two beams of light passed on the main road. The car slowed briefly before continuing. The taste of blood in his mouth made him realize he had bitten his cheek. He swallowed hard and pulled open the door to the staff room, determined to finish what he had started.

* * *

A battered safe with a key lock sat in the corner behind a cluttered desk. Fredrik accidentally knocked over a pile of papers, leaving muddy footprints as they scattered across the floor. His feet, cold and stiff, slid uncomfortably in the oversized sandals. He carefully tried the safe handle, but it didn't budge. Instinctively, he rummaged through the top drawer for a key. Finding nothing, he turned to the cash register, lifting out the bill tray. Beneath it, he discovered a small key. His hands trembled as he unlocked the safe and began pulling out bundles of bills, most wrapped with rubber bands. They were mainly euros.

The reversed roles at the crime scene were unsettling. Fredrik had no plans to become a full-time criminal.

The timer on his phone showed nineteen minutes had passed; it was time to go. He used a screwdriver to scratch new marks on the door frame and carefully wiped down the crowbar and wedge. After tossing the tools and wood pieces into the trunk, he slipped the money bag under the passenger seat and quickly changed shoes before pulling onto the main road.

The weight of the bag felt reassuring. As warmth filled the car, he returned to the cottage, reversing into the yard.

He unlocked the door and, despite his trembling hands, quickly stashed his tools and shoes inside. The night air hung thick, moisture clinging to every surface. The fan still hummed softly in the bedroom as he returned the crowbar to its hiding spot. He meticulously rinsed the plastic sandals in bleach, scrubbing away any trace of evidence, and wiped them down with wet wipes.

Exhaustion weighed heavily on Fredrik, pushing him dangerously close to the point where mistakes were made. He counted to a hundred, then backward, repeatedly to keep his mind sharp. Once satisfied with his work, he locked the door and drove toward the lighthouse. Upon reaching the parking lot, he turned off the engine and sat in the dark.

He used a few more wet wipes to pick up the sandals, giving them one final cleaning before tossing them into a nearby bin. As he did, a decision crystallized—this would be his first and last burglary. Fifty-two minutes had passed since he left his room.

Driving back to the hotel, he wiped the sweat from his face with the scarf, trying to steady his nerves. Two patrol cars passed as he was inching closer to the safety of his room.

CHAPTER TWENTY-FOUR

The man standing before Ziggy was next to die. His death was inevitable—a natural progression in a series of unfortunate events. Some people were destined to fail, and the man was one of them. Ziggy, on the other hand, had always been a winner.

The mild morning breeze had given way to solid gusts, whipping up the sand. Ziggy hated the sand. The woman who had once promised him the world had loved the damned sand. Too late, he realized she had been after nothing but money and fame—another loser. Most people started strong, brimming with promise and potential, but they slipped into their comfort zone somewhere along the way, trading ambition for mere hopes and wishes. They didn't believe in God yet sat around waiting for miracles.

The man before him had made his choice; he would soon take the final leap. Ziggy remained sharp and entirely in control, his senses heightened by the situation.

"Why? They'll find you. This bubble will burst," the man stammered.

Ziggy's patience was wearing thin. Without hesitation, he struck the man on the forehead with the butt of a gun. The man wavered, about to fall backward, but Ziggy seized his arm and pulled him close, gripping his leg as if in a twisted dance. A dance that would be his last.

A faint dawn battled against the dark clouds on the horizon. The people who hoped and prayed for miracles would soon awake to a new day.

Nothing had changed.

Yet.

CHAPTER TWENTY-FIVE
Tuesday, October 24

Forty-eight hours had passed since Moa's return from the turbine, and the tension surrounding Bernd's murder had reached a boiling point with the revelation of DNA evidence implicating Rasmus.

"Looks like everyone's here," Erik said, nodding towards Moa, Ylva, and the prosecutor, Anna.

His awkwardness was replaced with a focused urgency.

"As you know, Rasmus's DNA was found in Bernd's nail scrapings. Rasmus isn't answering his phone. As we speak, a patrol is going inside to see if there are any signs of him. We need to track down the USB drive that was found yesterday. Moa, do you have any updates?"

"Fredrik sent the file to the digital forensic team. He said it contained two maps—one showing plans to build houses near the protected beach Vallarna on the west coast and another detailing some man-made islands in the sea. He saved the file before handing the drive to Rasmus."

"Excellent," Erik said. "A forensic technician is never really off-duty. We need to recover the USB drive—there might be more data on it, like deleted files, which could be crucial."

Moa nodded, sensing the growing tension in the room as Ylva arranged her papers.

"Fredrik mentioned Rasmus seemed unusually restless," Moa added, sharing her little insight.

"I'll talk to Fredrik today when I head to Nordby," Ylva said. "There are still many unresolved questions in Rasmus's investigation."

"Rasmus's DNA is not enough, and we need witnesses and, more importantly, a clear motive. Finding Bernd's mobile or laptop would be our best bet, Anna added."

"We'll see what the day brings. Ylva, did you find anything else on Rasmus?" Erik asked.

Ylva leaned forward and said, "Rasmus mentioned someone within the municipality who received a dead bird in their letterbox but didn't want to report it. There should be some notes about it on his desk. This happened when discussions about various coastal projects were heating up, including the planned hotel near the nature reserve. I'll check his desk and see what I can find."

"Let's leave Rasmus for now," Erik said, shifting focus. "Anna, you mentioned something about an arrest warrant?"

"Yes. Casper Brix, a carpenter and owner of Brix Fix, oversees the expansion of The Pier Crown Hotel, which is Jan's property. According to Casper, Ingrid asked him to buy the lashing straps. Jan, who owns a sailboat, had given Ingrid a note with what he needed. Casper purchased them on Tuesday and left the straps in his van, planning to take them to the hotel the next day. Nothing unusual there. The van's back door was unlocked while he was on the job, and on Wednesday morning, the bag with the straps and a toolbox was gone. He didn't report it since it was a small loss and his fault for leaving the van unlocked."

Ylva, looking pleased, jotted down a quick note and said, "We released Casper. There was no reason to hold him any longer. Let's move on. A toothbrush was found in the cabin on Tora East; we're running the DNA test on that one. We also found a couple of fingerprints that matched those in the helicopter. The gum found matches Elis Fischer's DNA. The German police have his fingerprints and DNA on file and are as eager as we are to find him since his name has surfaced in an arms smuggling investigation."

"That's progress. We have a name, but why Rasmus?" Erik queried. "The pilot's apartment was spotless. Moa, do you have anything?"

"The bird in Bernd's mouth was a yellow bunting with a broken neck. There is no trace of fibers. That's all I have."

Moa ticked off something on her notepad. The meeting dragged on, with much of it rehashing known details. Everyone seemed to be waiting for a breakthrough. Ylva cleared her throat, looking at Moa as she spoke, "The boat found adrift belonged to Otto Axelgaard, a retiree. It was moored in Toft's marina, and Otto planned a last trip this weekend before the winter. I've also heard from Preben Hesselund—he's still in shock and receiving trauma counseling. He had nothing new to add but promised to reach out if he recalls anything useful. The door-knocking in the neighborhood has taken a massive amount of time, and no one seems to have seen or heard anything. I'm looking into the company Green Air, and I know Rasmus found some leads there. I suspect there might be a connection to the recent events here."

Ylva's phone rang, and her expression made everyone freeze. The radio crackled with information, sending a chill through the room. Ylva put down her phone and announced, "They've found Rasmus."

CHAPTER TWENTY-SIX

The break-in would likely haunt Fredrik for the rest of his life. He promised himself that once he got his life back on track, he would make a large donation to the zoo.

Trying to accept his actions, Fredrik spent the morning at the parking lot by the lighthouse. The sky was a heavy gray, with clouds threatening rain, and he hoped the weather would keep other visitors away. Standing tall against the stormy backdrop, the lighthouse had become his anchor in the recent chaos. Behind him, the vast, open landscape and the endless sea on the horizon offered a glimpse of something pure and beautiful amidst the ugliness of his life.

He parked at the far end of the lot, with a clear view of the lighthouse ahead and the sea stretching out to the left. With a traveler's curiosity, he stepped out of the car and inhaled deeply as if the salty air could cleanse him.

The narrow road to the lighthouse was still closed, with a sign indicating the gate would open at ten o'clock. As he walked back to his car, the only sound was the crunch of gravel beneath his feet.

He had caught a few hours of sleep after Tim let him in. Fredrik had made sure to inform everyone about his severe gunshot wound and the chronic pain that followed—letting as many people as possible know about his physical limitations was part of his plan.

Tim had dropped his macho act and offered Fredrik a cup of tea. But Fredrik, still trembling from the night's exertion, was eager to get back to his room. Though he would have liked to take the opportunity to chat with Tim, he settled for the reassurance that he was on his side. The loot was safely stashed under the car seat, and Lars's car had been parked outside the hotel when Fredrik returned. Where Lars had been at three in the morning was a mystery Fredrik might never solve. Nordby wasn't exactly known for its nightlife, especially not at that hour.

Fredrik reached into the bag and pulled out a bundle of banknotes, feeling the weight in his hand and the rough texture of the paper against his fingertips. The bundle was mainly made up of twenties and some five- and ten-euro notes. He slipped a few bills into his wallet, making a mental note to find a better hiding place for the money before the day ended.

A sudden flutter of wings startled him as a flock of birds flew from a nearby bush. Dark clouds loomed over the sea, casting long shadows as a car approached. Fredrik quickly hid the bag under the seat and reclined his chair as raindrops began splattering across the windshield. A white Volvo parked next to the information board, and as the door opened, Fredrik saw the lighthouse tour guide walking down the path. She unlocked the gate, and Fredrik peered through the misted window, regretting that he'd tossed the sandals in the trash bin earlier. Fatigue and exhaustion had dulled his judgment. A tall man stepped out of the Volvo, his hood pulled low over his head.

The man's movements were jerky, his posture stiff, and Fredrik immediately recognized the worn leather jacket. Rasmus. Fredrik's heart pounded in his chest as he watched Rasmus glance around, check his phone, and walk toward the lighthouse as the sky unleashed a torrent of rain. The tour guide was nowhere to be seen. Fredrik felt like a spectator in a film, detached and waiting for the director to tell him what to do next.

Don't get involved. It's not the time to call the police. *Go back to the hotel.*

His inner voice, usually reliable, urged him to leave. Fredrik started the car and reached for his phone but hesitated. Maybe things had changed overnight, and Rasmus was no longer a suspect.

The lighthouse stood starkly against the stormy sky, its white facade contrasting with the dark clouds. Sheets of rain pelted the sea, forming a white streak rapidly moving toward land. Fredrik opened the window and snapped a photo of the lighthouse, his mind uncertain.

A woman's voice pierced through the rain-soaked air. The lighthouse tour guide was running back and forth, her hands covering her mouth in horror.

Fredrik turned off the engine, leaped out of the car, and sprinted up the path. He met the woman halfway, her face twisted with terror, struggling to speak as tears welled up in her eyes.

Rasmus lay on the gravel at the base of the lighthouse. Instinctively, Fredrik switched to his role as a police officer and forensic technician.

One glance told him the grim truth: Rasmus had jumped from the lighthouse. His right leg was grotesquely twisted, the foot pointing inward at an unnatural angle. Fredrik grabbed the woman, who was trembling uncontrollably.

"I'm a police officer," he said, his voice steady. "What's your name?"

The woman stared at him, clearly surprised by the question.

"Pia," she finally replied.

"Pia," he repeated calmly, gently placing his hand on her shoulders. "I need you to stay here and keep your eyes on the path, okay? I'm going to check on the man."

Without waiting for her response, Fredrik turned her around and sprinted back to Rasmus. He found him lying on his back, his eyes open, his head twisted unnaturally— his neck broken. Fredrik's fingers searched for a pulse, but there was none. Blood trickled from Rasmus's nose, ears, and mouth, quickly washed away by the rain, which had begun to intensify. Pia's cries grew louder.

As Fredrik was about to return to her, something caught his eye—a fresh mark on Rasmus's forehead above his right eyebrow. It didn't align with the image of a fall. Fredrik scanned the gravel, searching for any traces of blood, but found none. Quickly, he pulled out his phone and snapped a photo of the mark. It looked like a blow from a blunt object. Moving closer, he noticed part of the forehead bone caved inward. His eyes swept over the low rosehip hedges surrounding the lighthouse. The only sounds were Pia's sobs and the relentless crash of the waves against the shore. Fredrik took a few more photos of Rasmus's body before hurrying back to Pia. He guided her into the nearby tourist office, one of two small buildings about thirty meters from the lighthouse. She looked around, disoriented, before collapsing into a chair by the window.

"Give me the keys to the gate. I'll lock it so no one can come in, and I'll call the police," Fredrik said.

With a trembling hand, Pia pointed to the desk behind the counter, where a set of keys lay next to her handbag. Fredrik grabbed an umbrella from the bag and headed back to the gate, dialing the emergency number. He explained the situation twice, ensuring they also sent an ambulance for Pia.

A distant rumble of thunder echoed across the sky as Fredrik returned to the office. Pia sat motionless, staring blankly ahead, a crumpled tissue in her hand. Her handbag had tipped over onto the floor.

"I've locked the gate," Fredrik said gently. "The ambulance and police are on their way. Someone will be here to help you soon."

"You said you were a police officer," Pia whispered, her voice trembling.

"I am, but I'm here on vacation."

Pia looked up at him, her hands still shaking. "He didn't buy a ticket. Is he... is he dead?"

"Unfortunately, yes," Fredrik replied softly.

"Death doesn't require a ticket," Pia murmured, the words sending a chill down Fredrik's spine despite his years on the job.

"Is there anyone I should call for you?" he asked, trying to be as gentle as possible.

Pia stared at the wall and shook her head.

"I'll be outside, keeping watch by the gate. I'm right here if you need anything," Fredrik assured her.

"Be careful," she whispered without looking at him.

The rain had eased up slightly as Fredrik returned to the lighthouse. When he reached Rasmus's body, he saw that it had shifted, now lying face down on the wet gravel.

CHAPTER TWENTY-SEVEN

Ziggy didn't get as high as expected. Nothing seemed to ease the stress. It was a dirty job, and someone had to do it. He was the only one who knew how and the only one who dared. The wet grass made him shiver. It was time to leave.

CHAPTER TWENTY-EIGHT

The first responders at the lighthouse were a two-officer patrol car. Fredrik presented his identification and interpreter badge, explaining that he was on vacation but had recently assisted Rasmus.

"We were close by," one of the officers said, stepping out of the car. "There was a break-in at the zoo last night. What are you doing out here in this weather?"

"I wanted to enjoy the silence, maybe take in the scenery. The rain caught me off guard, and I was about to head back to the hotel when I heard a scream."

He realized his explanation sounded almost too practiced. Together, they made their way toward the body.

"Where's the tour guide? Is there anyone else around who might have seen something?"

"She's in the tourist office, in shock. I helped her inside, and when I came back here, the body had been moved."

Fredrik pulled up the photos he'd taken earlier.

"I couldn't have been gone for more than three minutes. When I returned, he was lying face down. I checked his pulse, but he was already gone."

The officer sent his partner to check on Pia while he began cordoning off the area. He called for reinforcements, requesting a K-9 unit and forensic technicians.

"There are four cars in the parking lot. How did you get here?" the officer asked.

Fredrik pointed to the vehicles. "The blue Toyota is mine. The white Volvo belongs to Rasmus, and the other two must have arrived after I ran up here."

Before long, the area was awash with flashing blue lights. A patrol car remained in the parking lot, and soon, an ambulance and a forensic technician's van drove up the path toward the lighthouse. Moa and Erik approached, their expressions tense.

"Good thing you were here," Erik said with a sigh of relief.

"You'll never forget Friland," Moa added.

He recounted the events in detail, showing them his photos. Erik immediately called for a forensic pathologist and additional forensic technicians to the scene. Suicide was quickly ruled out, and the lighthouse area was declared a crime scene. Pia was taken care of and left with the ambulance.

Moa and Erik set up a tent to protect the body from the rain and facilitate their work.

"Head to the tourist office and give the patrol officers your statement," Erik instructed. "Send the photos to my phone, and then you can go. We'll be here for a while. There was also a break-in at the zoo. You didn't happen to pass by and see anything there, did you?"

Fredrik shook his head. "Unfortunately, I can't help you with that."

Now, in a coverall, Moa brushed a strand of hair from her face before pulling up the hood. "It was a professional job at the zoo," she said. "We'll investigate it later. The loot was about thirty-five thousand euros. We suspect someone close to the owners was involved—it usually is the case."

Fredrik's stomach tightened as the weight of his actions hit him. As Moa disappeared into the tent, he remembered he hadn't locked his car after hearing the scream.

Seeing his car within the cordon made him nauseous. The warmth inside the office was a welcome contrast to the cold sweat that had broken out across his skin, but it did little to steady his nerves. A police officer had taken Pia's seat.

"Ylva is on her way here and wants to speak with you," the officer informed him.

Fredrik instinctively placed a hand on his shoulder. "I just need to pop down to the car for my medication. I was shot in the line of duty."

The officer's expression softened. "Damn. And now you walk right into this mess."

Fredrik approached his car, trying to keep his steps light and casual.

"Leaving already?" the officer lifting the barricade tape asked as Fredrik approached.

"Not yet. I'm waiting for Ylva. I found Rasmus. I'm a police officer and interpreter—here on vacation."

"Quite the adventure vacation," the officer chuckled, and Fredrik forced a smile in return.

He glanced inside the car, his heart pounding as he scanned the floor for anything out of place. Nothing was visible under the seat. As the officer drew nearer, Fredrik quickly locked the doors and pulled a pack of pills from his pocket.

"Forgot these," he said, shaking the bottle lightly. "Got shot on duty recently."

* * *

Back in the tourist office, an eerie calm had settled around the lighthouse. Fredrik leaned against the wall, listening to the muffled voices outside. The door opened, and a medium-height woman with black glasses walked in. She was elegantly dressed in a white shirt under an exclusive black wool blazer with matching trousers, accented by a gray-patterned scarf.

"Fredrik Dal?" she asked.

Fredrik straightened up, shaking her firm hand.

"Ylva Moore," she introduced herself, pulling a chair up to the desk. She placed two reports before her, noting the date and time.

"We'll kill two birds with one stone," she said, her tone efficient. "I need to supplement part of the information on Bernd's murder as well."

Ylva seemed to be the antithesis of Rasmus. As Fredrik recounted how he had met Rasmus at an event in Oslo years ago, why he was in Nordby on vacation, and how he had found the USB drive on the beach, Ylva listened intently.

"Moa mentioned the drive and that you sent the files. That's good. We're still hoping to find the drive itself."

"Rasmus told me to delete the file, but I didn't. I also took a photo of the drive before handing it over. I'll send it to you now," Fredrik said, pulling out his phone.

"Well done. Having a forensic technician as a witness is a rare stroke of luck in any investigation."

"Rasmus seemed restless," Fredrik continued. "He kept checking his phone and looked unusually scruffy."

Ylva nodded, a faint smile tugging at the corner of her mouth. "Rasmus was often a bit scruffy, but maybe more so lately. His girlfriend recently broke up with him; perhaps that has something to do with it. But he was one of our best. We haven't found anything else on the beach, so the information on the drive may not be related to Bernd at all."

"Something personal?" Fredrik asked, clinging to the hope that Rasmus had been in the wrong place at the wrong time.

"It's possible," Ylva replied, her expression thoughtful.

CHAPTER TWENTY-NINE

The rain drummed against the tent as Fredrik's observation confirmed their conclusion: Rasmus hadn't jumped from the lighthouse willingly.

Moa steeled herself, slipping into the role she needed to keep going. Erik wiped his eyes with the back of his hand.

"We'll press on and find the evidence that leads us to the truth," Moa said, trying to believe her own words.

"Will you take the photos while I document the findings?" Erik asked, his voice steady despite the tension.

They worked swiftly, knowing they had to pick up the pace. The investigation had been dragging, and the German police were demanding answers to Bernd's murder.

"He took a blow to the forehead before he went over," Erik stated, pointing to a fresh mark.

A dog barked in the distance, shattering the silence.

"Maybe they've picked up a trail?" Moa suggested. "Whoever's behind this must have been hiding nearby, watching Fredrik enter the tourist office."

She shuddered at the thought of Fredrik being next to a potential killer. He looked fragile and lost, yet something about him stirred a longing within her.

"And someone would've had to come down here to move the body?" Erik suggested.

"Or the same person who hit him. Maybe there was a struggle, and Rasmus fell—or was pushed? This would take at least two people, wouldn't it?"

"Possibly," Erik conceded.

"But why?" Moa wondered aloud. "It feels like someone's playing with us, or maybe there's a psychopath at large," she added.

Rasmus's dirty leather jacket was unbuttoned, revealing a gray hoodie and a grimy T-shirt underneath. His clothes were disheveled, exposing a couple of ribs. Moa searched his pockets and found his phone. Her fingers brushed against something small and round in the inner pocket of his jacket. When she pulled it out, her heart skipped a beat—a dead bird. Erik's face drained of color.

"What the hell!"

The dead bird, likely the same species as the one found in Bernd Jung's mouth, confirmed their theory that Rasmus hadn't committed suicide.

We are lucky Fredrik was here," Erik said as he stood up. He looked uncertain, shifting his weight from one leg to another as he peered out of the tent.

"Let's check out the beacon," Moa said, closing her bag and pulling off her face mask.

The air was thick and stifling, and a dull ache settled between her temples. She drained her water bottle, noticing Erik's frozen stance and pallor. The memory of the helicopter ride to the turbine flashed through her mind— Erik's fear of heights, his career teetering on the edge. He had a house in an affluent area, two children, and a wife who worked part-time and enjoyed expensive vacations.

"I'll go alone," Moa said firmly. "You need to seek professional help for your fear of heights. I can't cover for you anymore. Dismantle the tent so I can get a clear view of the scene."

Erik hesitated, closed his eyes briefly, and nodded.

Moa grabbed her camera and bag, changed her shoe covers, and began the ascent. Her footsteps echoed on the damp staircase, the air heavy with the scent of seawater and mold. She kept close to the wall, one hand steadying herself as she climbed. At step forty-seven, she paused to catch her breath, switching the bag to her other hand before continuing slowly.

The staircase revealed nothing out of the ordinary. A clean crime scene hinted at the work of multiple perpetrators—quick, calculated, and precise. Rasmus couldn't have been struck elsewhere, driven here, and willingly jumped. He would've known that the DNA evidence alone wouldn't be enough to convict him. There had to be more to this, something no one else knew. According to Fredrik, Rasmus had approached the lighthouse calmly, showing no signs of distress. Someone must have been waiting for him, possibly arranging a meeting at the lighthouse, sneaking in when the tour guide's attention was diverted—someone familiar with the area.

Below, Erik had already dismantled the tent. Moa pulled out her phone and called him.

"Can you step out of the way? I need to take some shots, and I don't want you in them."

She quickly snapped a photo, watching as Erik moved out of frame. He owed her for this. If things got messy, a picture of him could be a good backup. Officially, two forensic technicians should work on a crime scene together.

Despite the grim setting, the area was eerily serene, as if time stood still and nothing terrible had happened. The waist-high ledge circling the top of the lighthouse made it all too easy for someone to take a fatal leap.

They had reinforced the upper part by adding a metal rib panel, adding an extra ten centimeters of height. Moa crouched down, dusting the panel for fingerprints. Given the lighthouse's steady flow of visitors, she knew she'd find plenty even in winter.

She paused, staring at the ledge, trying to piece together the sequence of events. It wouldn't have taken much to push Rasmus over the edge. Most likely, he had been struck on the forehead while resisting, causing him to stagger before being quickly shoved. The bird could have been stuffed into his pocket while he lay on the ground.

Rasmus's body would be taken away soon. Moa felt her eyes sting with tears. The closure of the zipper on the body bag marked the definitive end. Any hope the person might still be alive was gone. She made her way down the stairs slowly.

"They found a tire track," Erik said, gesturing toward the dunes covered in long, yellowed grass.

"I'll head inside to see if Ylva has any updates," Moa replied. "And to warm my hands for a bit."

"We have clearance to collect as much evidence we think is valuable," Erik added.

"Good to know there won't be any budget cuts on a murder investigation," she said, with a trace of irony.

As she turned away, the ice-cold rain blended in with her tears.

CHAPTER THIRTY

A damp, sour smell of wet clothes permeated the small tourist office. A police officer walked in, holding the hand of a little boy whose jacket was soaked, with his red hair plastered to his forehead.

"We found him in a bunker on the beach. He might have seen something," the officer said, guiding the boy to the chair next to Fredrik's before stepping back into the rain.

The boy slumped into the chair, trying to make himself as small as possible, his eyes fixed on the floor, and he was on the verge of tears.

Ylva broke the silence by pulling out a roll of toilet paper.

"It's not much, but it might help a bit," she said gently, tearing off a long strip. "I'm Ylva, a police officer, though I'm not in uniform today. Why don't you remove your wet jacket, and we can hang it over the chair to dry? What's your name?"

The boy glanced at Ylva and Fredrik, wiping his nose with the paper before slipping off his jacket.

"Max. I saw you," he said, fixing his gaze at Fredrik.

His eyes were light and innocent blue, but Fredrik could tell they had already seen too much for someone so young. Max looked about ten years old—an age where he should have been in school, not alone in a German war bunker.

"How old are you?" Ylva asked. Max continued wiping his face and blowing his nose. Three scratches marked his forearm. His shirt was stained, and blades of grass clung to his jeans. He held up eight fingers, his eyes scanning the room warily.

"What are you doing out here? Shouldn't you be in school?" Ylva asked.

Max shrugged, blowing his nose again, and avoided eye contact.

"What were you doing there?" she continued, her tone soft but probing.

"Nothing special," he muttered.

"Where do you live? We'll take you home."

Freckles dotted his cheeks as Max swung his legs, his once-white sneakers now caked with mud and sand. One shoelace had come undone, trailing on the floor.

"I saw him sitting in his car, flipping through a notebook," Max said, pointing at Fredrik. "I thought about sneaking up to see what he was doing, but then it started raining, so I stayed in the bunker. Is he a criminal?"

Ylva suppressed a smile. "He's not a criminal, Max. Where do you live? Can we call your mum?"

Tears welled up in Max's eyes. Ylva paused, giving him a moment to gather himself as he blew his nose again.

Fredrik found a bottle of Coca-Cola in the pantry's fridge.

"Want to share this?" he offered.

Max looked at Ylva, seeking permission.

"I'll have a sip, too," she said, smiling to reassure him.

The bottle hissed as Fredrik twisted off the cap. Max took a drink in silence, his gaze drifting toward the desk.

"How long have you been in the bunker?" Ylva asked, her voice calm and steady.

"Since eight," Max replied. "I saw the woman who sells tickets. She had a bicycle. Then it rained. After that, some cars came up and turned around. Then he came."

Max glanced at Fredrik and downed the rest of his drink.

"Have you eaten?" Fredrik asked. Max shook his head and held out the empty glass. Fredrik poured more Coca-Cola, watching as the boy drank quickly.

It was nearing lunchtime, and Fredrik felt the exhaustion from yesterday's events weighing heavily on him. His jacket was soaked, and he struggled to remove it, the cold, damp fabric clinging to his shoulders despite the warmth of the office. Max ruffled his wet hair, looking as drained as Fredrik felt.

Fredrik wasn't involved in the investigation and needed to return to the hotel for a hot shower.

"Do you come here often?" Ylva asked.

The question seemed to shift something in Max. His expression darkened as he crossed his legs, leaned back in the chair, and folded his arms defensively.

"Maybe," he muttered.

He picked up his phone, and Fredrik couldn't help but notice the dirt on Max's pants and shoes. The boy must be hungry and tired. Max's fingers moved swiftly across the screen as he clutched the phone like a lifeline.

"Can we help you call someone? Is anyone home for you now?" Ylva's voice took on a firmer edge, laced with concern.

"I took some photos of him. Does that make me a suspect?" Max's words hit like a punch to the gut. Fredrik felt his legs go numb, adrenaline coursing through him like sharp needles. He tried to picture the angle from which Max could have seen the parking lot and the lighthouse. Ylva chuckled.

"You're not a suspect, Max. Neither you nor Fredrik has done anything wrong."

"I'm skipping school," Max said, sitting up straight, almost proud of the attention he was getting.

He held out his phone, and Fredrik saw an image of himself, head down, sitting in the car. If Max had gotten closer and positioned himself on the dune by the parking lot, he could have zoomed in on the bundle of banknotes.

"He looked suspicious, sitting alone in his car so early in the morning," Max added.

Ylva looked puzzled at Fredrik as Max's words lingered in the air.

I saw you.

Fredrik's unease deepened. He didn't like this—didn't like Max.

The faint light that had trickled through the window vanished abruptly. The sky darkened, and rain pounded against the glass as lightning streaked across the sky like a jagged scar. Max jumped down to the floor, getting more mud on his pants. The thunder rattled the windowpanes, and the boy started to cry. Fredrik instinctively reached out, and though Max hesitated at first, he soon melted into Fredrik's arms. The dampness from Max's pants seeped through Fredrik's. It was as if a dam had burst, and all the emotions Max had held back came pouring out.

"Vandflodvej," Max sobbed. "Mom is at work. They fight. I'm scared."

Fredrik held Max tightly, gently rocking him as another flash of lightning split the sky.

"I saw you," Max repeated through his tears. "You looked scared. That's all I saw. I swear."

Max's sniffling filled the room as the relentless rain hammered down, isolating them from the outside world. Fredrik's hunger gnawed at him, his exhaustion deepening as Max clung to his sore shoulder. Ylva walked to the door, peering out before shutting it against the downpour.

"Who are you afraid of? Is it someone at home?" Fredrik's question made Max cry harder, his body tensing.

"The others. At school. Filming everything. You wouldn't understand."

Max sniffled. He breathed more calmly and seemed to relax as the rain subsided.

Ylva sided with Max and called his mom, who promised to come and pick up her son. In the meantime, Max went down to the parking lot with the police officers and waited in one of the police cars.

Fredrik stood up, feeling dizzy, gripping the back of his chair for support.

"You look like you've been through the wringer. Moa mentioned your injury," Ylva said. "You can leave now if you—"

The door swung open, and Moa entered as the body of Rasmus was being wheeled out. Fredrik caught a glimpse of the gray body bag.

"I was supposed to grab a beer with Rasmus last night, but it didn't happen. 'There will be a lot happening here'—that's the last thing he said. I wonder what he meant by that."

Erik held something familiar in his hand.

"Sandals," he said. "Crocs. Found them on the beach. Bit late in the season to be wearing these."

"What size?" Moa asked.

Erik flipped the orange shoes. "Size forty-seven."

"Same size as Rasmus," she noted. "Let's bag them."

Phones began ringing, and Ylva said, "This is too much. I need a quiet place and something to eat. Now."

She looked at Fredrik, who was trying to clean the mud from his pants, his mind racing. He'd cleaned those sandals meticulously—how did they end up on the beach?

"Café Lykken," Moa suggested, taking charge. "You're coming with us."

She glanced at Fredrik before heading out the door. Fredrik turned his back on the lighthouse, determined not to return anytime soon. A thin voice echoed in his mind: I saw you. You were flipping through a notebook.

I saw you.

As they left the office, the K-9 unit arrived.

"We found a crowbar in the grass behind the lighthouse," one officer reported.

CHAPTER THIRTY-ONE

During Fredrik's short drive from the lighthouse to Café Lykken, his thoughts spiraled about fate playing a trick on him. Could the crowbar they found behind the lighthouse be the one from his cottage? Did anyone know? He was eager to go and check if the crowbar was still where he had left it.

"I don't like any of this," Ylva said. She twisted the smooth silver ring on her left finger, her unease evident.

"There's no logical connection between Rasmus, plastic sandals, and a crowbar," Moa added. "It must be a coincidence. No point in speculating now."

"Would Rasmus have hit himself with the crowbar?" Erik asked, downing a glass of water and quickly pouring another.

"Someone must have been waiting for him at the lighthouse," Moa suggested.

"Most likely," Ylva agreed.

Fredrik shuddered at the thought of someone hiding in the shadows, watching him approach Rasmus—someone who intended to murder Rasmus and stage it as a suicide. This person saw Fredrik taking photos, fully aware he would report it to the police.

"If there's blood on that crowbar, we can't dismiss the possibility it was used in the attack," Ylva said. "How long does running down a hundred and seventy steps take?"

Ylva's gaze shifted between Erik and Moa, curiosity and concern mingling in her eyes.

"I'd estimate about a minute, maybe forty-five seconds if they're really fit," Moa speculated. "I used to train on stairs a lot before my knees started to hurt. It will take much longer if you carry something heavy or awkward."

"And the railing up there is only waist-high," Erik pointed out.

"As I mentioned earlier at the meeting, I found notes on Rasmus's desk about a dead bird sent to someone in the municipality," Ylva said. "Turns out it was Henning Hager. He received an anonymous threat but didn't want to report it. I'll be talking to him. He's in Switzerland right now but due back tonight."

Both Moa and Erik exchanged surprised glances. Ylva took a bite of her food and continued, "Rasmus's ex called me last week—just a courtesy call; we've known each other for a while. She mentioned she was worried about him. Said he'd lost weight, buried himself in work, and barely saw his friends. At this point, I don't know what to believe. We also know Rasmus was licensed to fly a helicopter."

127

"And the dead bird in his pocket strengthens the theory that Rasmus's death might be tied to Bernd's murder," Moa added.

Ylva's phone, which had been quiet, suddenly buzzed, and her expression suggested that a few puzzle pieces were about to fall into place.

"The German police found messages from Tim Klein on Bernd Jung's Viber account," Ylva said. "Tim mentioned he had some spare time on Friday, and they agreed to meet."

"Why did it take them so long to access his account?" Moa muttered.

"If we had found his phone, it would have been much easier," Ylva said, frustration evident in her voice. "Apparently, Bernd had three user accounts on his laptop and had logged out of all his social media—very old-school. It will be interesting to hear what excuse Tim comes up with. It's time to bring him in."

"Tim runs at the lighthouse," Fredrik added. "He trains there with Jan. He mentioned it yesterday, and it didn't sound like his usual bragging."

Ylva nodded thoughtfully and said, "Interesting."

Silence fell over the table as everyone seemed equally tired. Regardless of fatigue, the determination to move forward persisted.

Ylva's phone buzzed again. She listened with a pained expression as a distressed voice seeped out, ending the call with a weary sigh.

"Henning Hager's secretary," she explained. "They're eager to have the cordon at the lighthouse removed."

Moa chuckled, shaking her head. "Serious crimes disrupt the tourist idyll," she said.

"Jan's dad?" Fredrik asked.

"Yeah," Moa replied. "He's got friends in high places and plenty of money. But police work isn't for sale."

"I've got a lot to do," Ylva said, unsuccessfully trying to catch someone's attention to ask for the check.

* * *

As Fredrik shut the car door behind him, he finally found the quiet he had been craving all morning. But it wasn't the peace of mind he had imagined. Ylva, Erik, and Moa left for the station, leaving Fredrik alone with the thirty-five thousand euros hidden under his car seat—money that needed to be dealt with sooner rather than later. But how?

CHAPTER THIRTY-TWO

Ziggy shut the car door with a thud and started the engine. Warm air quickly enveloped him, turning the car into a temporary refuge. He returned the missed call, his hands still trembling.

The voice on the other end was sharp, "Did you get the green light? We're waiting."

"In a couple of days," Ziggy replied, directing the heater toward his frozen body, trying to shake off the chill.

"We're holding off the next payment. You know what happens if you don't deliver."

Ziggy didn't need to check his bank account to know he was already in deep shit. He was so close.

Another craving surged through his body. He needed to quell the desire, yet, at the same time, he wanted to keep a clear head.

He switched off the phone, cursing under his breath.

Crap

No one would stop him now. This time, he would make even bigger headlines. They had no idea who they were dealing with—but soon, they would. A grin spread across his face.

CHAPTER THIRTY-THREE

Moa braced herself to face a new crime scene.

"What took you so long? We can't remain closed all day," the man grumbled.

He owned the zoo and was agitated, worried about the customers waiting outside and the money he was losing by the minute.

"We got here as fast as we could," Erik replied, his tone firm.

Moa's eyes swept the area, searching for surveillance cameras, but none were in sight. The connection between two murders and a break-in seemed tenuous at best, but given the circumstances, she knew better than to dismiss anything.

"Five bolts on the door—they're possibly handling cash here. Whoever did this knew exactly what they were doing," Erik remarked. "I hate to admit it, but I've got to give them credit. Well done."

He handed the camera to Moa.

"It doesn't add up," she said, examining the door frame where someone had tried to scratch out evidence. "They were sloppy with the cover-up. And yet, someone knew exactly where to find the key and what was in the safe."

"This is one of the cleanest crime scenes I've ever seen," Erik noted, a hint of suspicion in his voice. "I wouldn't be surprised if a security guard or a police officer was involved. I would suggest looking into the relatives—maybe there's a connection in the force."

Moa pointed to the muddy footprints on the floor, the distinctive pattern instantly recognizable.

"The shoe prints aren't hard to identify."

"Crocs. Looks like a size forty-seven," Erik observed, his voice trailing off as he connected the dots. "The same size as the ones found at the lighthouse. Could it be Rasmus?"

Erik hesitated, the weight of the implications settling over them both.

Could Rasmus have been desperate enough to break in, looking for money? As a prime suspect, perhaps he was planning his escape from the islands. But Moa couldn't shake the image of Fredrik from her mind—he had gone home before midnight, pale and clearly in pain, but had stumbled into a series of strange coincidences. And he knew Rasmus from before. Could they have been in this together?

The entrance and staff room were quickly dusted with black powder, but the crime scene was so meticulously cleaned that finding any usable fingerprints seemed unlikely. The only hope was that fatigue might have caused the culprits to slip up.

Moa and Erik managed to lift a couple of partial prints. Erik's phone rang as they were about to head back to the station.

"Ylva wants to know when we'll be done. It's not urgent, but she and Anna are waiting at the station. They found Bernd Jung's mobile and the USB drive in Rasmus's apartment. They're examining them now."

Moa froze mid-motion. The murder of Bernd required careful planning and significant resources. Could Rasmus have been the mastermind? It would have taken a lot of money to pull it off—money someone like Rasmus might have been desperate for. Or was he a pawn in a larger scheme? Until now, Moa had resisted the idea that one of their own could be involved in something so dark. But with every new piece of evidence, that denial was slipping away.

CHAPTER THIRTY-FOUR

Fredrik entered the hotel reception, his legs stiff and aching from the day's ordeal. He spotted Casper, the carpenter, engaged in conversation with Ingrid. Their laughter and fragmented words floated his way: something about a door, tools, and a theft.

Earlier, Fredrik had returned to the cabin, hiding some of the stolen cash beneath a stack of stone slabs in the yard. He knew driving around with a bag of money wasn't a good idea. Irene's photo flashed on his phone, and he quickly declined the call. Casper turned as Fredrik approached, his work overalls embroidered with the name "Brix Fix." Sawdust clung to one leg, and paint specks dotted his boots.

"So, you're staying here?" Casper asked.

Ingrid's eyes locked onto Fredrik, her curiosity sharp.

He couldn't shake the feeling that Casper knew more than he was letting on—about the late-night escapade, the burglary, maybe even the cash. And what about Ingrid? Was she in on it, too?

"Do you two know each other?" Ingrid asked, her curiosity growing.

Casper ignored the question, leaving Fredrik to wonder if this was all part of a much larger game.

"We've met," Fredrik said, searching for the right words. They shared nothing beyond a broken wall.

"Heard there's been some drama around here," Casper added, lifting his cap and scratching his head. "You might want to stay inside at night. You never know what could happen."

Casper chuckled, but Ingrid scowled. Fredrik gave up trying to read her.

"It's some lunatic," she said. "Not someone from the neighborhood."

When Fredrik closed the door to his room, he immediately sensed something was off. His suitcase lid was slightly ajar, not how he'd left it. Maybe Violeta had accidentally nudged it while cleaning, but it didn't sit right. Once neatly tucked inside, the magazines and his to-do list were now misplaced atop two folded shirts.

He pulled out his laptop from the case, noting it was warm, and saw the login screen displayed. Someone had attempted to access his computer. A wave of unease washed over him as he scanned the room, half-expecting to find someone lurking in the shadows. The space that had once felt like a sanctuary now seemed tainted. His wet jacket hung limply over a chair, reminding him to buy a new one—something he could easily afford. Irene's call could wait, but guilt gnawed at him for not speaking to Dennis all day.

As he reached to unplug his phone, a message lit up the screen. The number was hidden.

I know something.

Fredrik spun around once more, his nerves on edge. The room was eerily quiet and empty, but the sound of footsteps echoed from the corridor. They slowed, stopping right outside his door. Someone knew what? His heart raced as a light knock broke the silence. A moment later, the soft hum of a key card was followed by the door swinging open.

"Oh, sorry," Violeta said, startled, mirroring Fredrik's unease. "Your pants," she continued, holding out his jeans.

He tried to smile, but Violeta still seemed anxious, as if she had more on her mind.

"Thanks," Fredrik said, taking the jeans.

She hesitated, words seemingly on the tip of her tongue, but quickly retreated. Fredrik watched her almost curtsy before leaving the room, her nervousness lingering.

Fredrik was drawn to a tag sticking out from the duvet cover. The plush duvet and pillow offered a small comfort amid his turmoil. He knew he would need to buy fresh bedding and towels once he returned to the cottage.

He tugged at the tag and read: *Friland White Pearl 90% white goose down, 10% white goose feathers.* On impulse, he snapped a photo of it.

* * *

Outside, he unexpectedly bumped into Lars. For once, he seemed inclined to chat and stopped.

"Can't sleep either?" he asked.

Fredrik found it hard to picture Lars as a chef; he looked more like a small-town bar owner with a penchant for afternoon cocaine. When Lars smiled, a gap in his front teeth became visible.

"I saw you last night," Lars said, his words hanging in the cool air.

Fredrik's confusion must have shown on his face because Lars continued, "I have trouble sleeping too. I was heading to Toft late last night. To a nightclub. I saw you on the road."

Had everyone in the area seen him that night?

"I drive around when the pain is at its worst," Fredrik explained. "I got shot in the line of duty."

Lars's cold, macho gaze softened. Even his shoulders slumped. "Holy crap. On duty, huh?"

"I'm a forensic technician."

"Shit. Sorry to hear that. So, that's why you were hanging around the cops. I saw you up at the restaurant on the main road one day. Good timing, though. They seem to need a bit of help around here. I'm Lars, though you probably don't recognize me."

"Sorry, I'm from the mainland, so I'm unfamiliar with the locals here on the islands. But Rasmus mentioned something about you."

Lars glanced around nervously; his pupils dilated as he looked up at the sky where a break in the clouds let through a sliver of light. Fredrik couldn't help but search his nostrils for any traces of white powder.

Before he knew it, he had somehow agreed to have a beer with Lars at the end of the week without fully understanding how it had happened.

CHAPTER THIRTY-FIVE

Moa locked the front door; it was late, and she was hungry. When she was about to raid the kitchen, Erik called.

"Haven't you gone home yet?" Moa asked.

"I'm finally heading home; I got stuck clearing my desk. They recovered the deleted files on the USB drive Fredrik found. There were photos of Tim Klein."

"Maybe we're close to a solution. Great."

She took a deep breath, trying to ease the tension in her body.

"But that's not why I called," Erik continued, his tone more serious. "I wanted to warn you—be extra vigilant. Ylva found a dead bird taped to her windshield. Keep your eyes open."

Moa's hunger turned into a dull headache. She washed down two painkillers and found a packet of biscuits in the kitchen cabinet. Despite the drawn blinds and her

Walther semi-automatic safely tucked away, a nagging unease settled over her. She caught herself scanning the room, searching for something out of place.

Doubt began creeping into her thoughts. Could she trust anyone around her? A long, hot shower might help chase away the mounting paranoia.

A knock echoed through the silence when she placed the last dish in the dishwasher. With biscuit crumbs still on her lips, she peered through the peephole and saw a young courier she recognized. Relieved, she opened the door.

"A delivery for Moa Bakke."

Her birthday was approaching. Maybe someone had remembered. Curiously, she sat down on the sofa and quickly unwrapped the parcel.

Inside was a small wooden box decorated with pink details on the lid. It was carefully wrapped in bubble wrap. She searched for a card but found none. Hesitation gripped her—was it safe to open?

Slowly, she lifted the lid, half-expecting something sinister. Instead, music began to play, and a ballerina appeared, spinning around on a mirror. The ballerina was missing her head.

CHAPTER THIRTY-SIX

Fredrik was about to head out for dinner when his phone buzzed. It was Moa.

"Can you come?" Her voice trembled, and he could hear a faint sniffle.

"I'm on my way. Are you hurt?"

"Someone's trying to scare me. It's not just me. I don't know how much more of this I can take."

The road from Nordby to Toft felt endless, stretching longer with every turn.

When Moa opened the door, her tear-streaked face revealed she had been crying. On the coffee table sat an open box.

"I got a delivery from DHL," she said, her voice shaky. "My birthday's coming up, so I thought it might be a gift."

She slipped on a pair of gloves and lifted the lid. The sight inside made Fredrik's skin crawl.

"Ylva found a dead bird on her windshield," Moa continued, pacing to the window and fidgeting with the already-closed blinds. "I don't know the details. Erik called me. I'm exhausted, hungry, freezing, and all I want is to sleep."

Fredrik moved closer, placing his hands gently on her shoulders. "Have you received any other messages? Any threats?"

She leaned into him, her body softening slightly as if his presence brought relief.

"Not yet."

"You can stay at my place tonight," Fredrik offered, aware of how childish it sounded.

Moa turned to him, her eyes still holding a spark of mischief despite the exhaustion, desperation, and fear that had clouded them.

"Are you allowed to bring a woman to your room?" she teased, wiping a mascara smudge from her cheek.

He leaned in close, whispering in her ear, "I can sneak you in through the back door. I'm a cop."

She turned to face him fully, wrapping her arms around his neck and resting her head against his chest. Fredrik gently stroked her back.

"I don't want you to be alone tonight," he murmured.

She pulled back slightly, her eyes searching the room as if lost in thought, tears shimmering in her eyes. "It's all too much," she admitted. "Right now, I feel vulnerable. Have you eaten?"

She pressed herself closer to him, shivering as if trying to draw warmth from his presence. He wanted to tell her everything would be alright, that he was her rock and would always keep her safe.

"Come with me," he insisted, his voice firm. "I mean it."

Moa let out a soft chuckle. "And I'm supposed to feel safe in a hotel where the night porter is currently in custody?"

"There are a few other colorful guests," Fredrik added.

"Do tell," she said, her interest piqued.

"There's Lars Gaard, the most famous chef in Friland, who stays out late and has dilated pupils. And a group of Japanese women swarming around Jan, a cleaner who might be a petty thief and snooping through my things. And finally, there's me, a gunshot-wounded cop here to protect you."

Moa smiled, but her expression changed as her phone beeped. Her face went pale as she read the message. Without a word, she handed the phone to Fredrik, her hand trembling slightly. It was a message from Erik.

Found a doll with no eyes stuffed in the mailbox. My youngest discovered it. Be careful.

She froze, her expression hardening as she slipped back into police mode. Without a word, she called the station, calmly reporting the incident and requesting a patrol to pick up the music box.

Fredrik quietly helped her gather clothes, packing them into a bag as Moa moved methodically through her home. She checked windows and doors, poured out old milk, and tied up the garbage bag, her movements precise and controlled.

The patrol arrived, collected the music box, jotted down their report, and vanished into the night. As they left, Moa's fear morphed into a simmering anger. She called Erik and Ylva, relayed the events, and told them where she would stay.

"I can handle a lot," she told Fredrik, pacing the living room. "Stress, messy crime scenes, collecting evidence from dismembered bodies, stepping in vomit and maggots. But when someone invades my private life, I get furious."

Fredrik's phone screen lit up again with the same cryptic message.

I know something.

"We're leaving now," Moa announced. "A few of the officers at the lighthouse this morning received strange messages, too. Staying here tonight is pointless; I won't be able to sleep. I've never heard of forensic technicians receiving threats."

She looked around the room, her gaze lingering on the familiar surroundings as if saying goodbye. After checking all the windows again, she locked the front door and activated the alarm.

"See you there," she said, her voice tinged with determination.

"I'll be right behind you," Fredrik replied.

Moa opened her car door, pausing momentarily to glance back at the house, her expression tinged with sadness as though she were leaving something behind.

CHAPTER THIRTY-SEVEN

Neither Jan nor Ingrid was around when Fredrik and Moa arrived at the hotel. Hanna eyed Moa's bag with curiosity but held back from asking questions; instead, she said, "Ingrid and Jan left for Toft with the Japanese group. You missed them by about fifteen minutes."

"I'm staying here tonight with Fredrik," Moa said, her voice steady. "I've received a threat."

Hanna's expression softened with concern as she stepped closer.

"I liked Rasmus. He was thorough and competent. We've already had a couple of cancellations because of everything that's happened, and we were expecting a honeymoon couple in the suite this weekend. We'll be bringing in a security guard later, and we'll keep the doors locked. Do you need anything? More pillows?"

Moa glanced at Fredrik, and for a moment, an unspoken connection sparked between them, taking him back to teenage summer camps—sneaking around with flashlights, the sound of giggles from the girls' tents, card games, mosquitoes, and the absence of worry about the future.

"We'll let you know if we need anything," he replied as they headed for the stairs.

"Welcome," he said to Moa as he opened the door to his room.

"Who went through your bags? The cleaner?"

"I wouldn't be surprised. She probably suspects I've noticed and tried to cover it up with small talk about the latest news as if I didn't already know. But she's been helpful. Maybe she's bored with so little to do. I doubt it'll get any better."

* * *

Later, they found themselves at the cozy restaurant Moa had suggested. The rustic wooden floors and candlelight created a warm, intimate atmosphere.

"It's like fate is pushing us together," Moa remarked.

"I don't mind."

"It's been a long day. I should have eaten hours ago, and there's so much I want to talk to you about," she said, her tone softer. "But maybe another day."

Despite Fredrik's curiosity and growing desire to be a part of Moa's life, he settled for light conversation. She had been through enough today, with her world turned upside down.

The rich scent of herbs filled the air, making his mouth water. A man walked in and nodded at Fredrik.

"Already making friends here?" Moa teased.

"I ran into him outside a store earlier. We chatted about the weather. He's got a nice dog."

Moa leaned in slightly and said, "We're convinced Rasmus was murdered. The mark on his forehead was fresh. Good job photographing it. Max's mother contacted us—she said her son might have seen someone enter the lighthouse before Rasmus arrived."

"That's impossible. I was there, and I didn't see anyone... although I might have looked away. Who knows?"

"Max will be interviewed tomorrow. It looks less likely that Rasmus jumped willingly. Someone could have snuck up, hit him on the head, and staged the scene."

"But his DNA was found on Bernd's body, which could point toward suicide. If Rasmus were convicted, his career would be over. It's a tough situation to escape. The only explanation that comes to mind is if they had a secret relationship, but that seems far-fetched."

Somewhere in the back of his mind, a scenario began to form—a vague, blurry image that he couldn't quite piece together.

Moa took a few bites of her salmon, though it seemed she was forcing herself to eat.

"Tell me about your cottage," she asked.

"My dad bought it about ten years ago as an investment. He doesn't have much time to look after it."

"Where is it?"

"Kystvej. Number forty-three."

"Jan has a cottage there."

A pang of jealousy settled under Fredrik's ribs.

Moa's expression grew serious. "He was supposed to get married about twenty years ago. She was Austrian. They talked about having kids. I remember her because my friend's family had a summer cottage nearby. We used to pass Jan's place when we took the shortcut to buy sweets. His fiancée, Gisela, was going to Vegavik to visit her brother, who worked at the oil terminal. Jan drove her to the bus stop. She never made it. Gisela Rebsdorf," she added quietly.

"Tragic," Fredrik muttered.

"She was seen getting on the bus. A witness remembers Jan standing there, watching as it pulled away from the station in Toft. But somewhere between Stackaby and Vegavik, she disappeared. Since then, he's barely been to the cottage. I doubt Ingrid likes staying there. His life hasn't been easy."

They paid and left the restaurant, walking back to the hotel.

"Do you snore?" Moa asked.

"Maybe if I'm really tired. Do you?"

"I hope not. There's something you should know, though. I lost my hair due to stress, so I wear a wig."

Fredrik nodded, taking it in. While Moa took a shower, he opened Facebook. Rasmus's profile was still there as if nothing had happened.

His last update was a quote: "Avoid missing something by always longing for something new." A dead man's final words had gotten three likes.

Fredrik scrolled through the news feed, an endless parade of curated lives: a man proudly posing with his new car, a woman flaunting oversized lips, perfectly arranged shopping bags, two children lost in a pile of toys, and a champagne glass raised against a Stockholm sunset. His life was a far cry from the picture-perfect world of social media.

The notification icon was the usual red, but he didn't have the energy or interest to sift through who liked what or whose birthday it was. Instead, he sent a quick message to Dennis, expressing how proud he was of him.

Moa emerged from the bathroom, a towel wrapped around her body, her wig clutched in one hand. She paced the room nervously before sinking into the armchair.

"You're beautiful," Fredrik said.

Outside, the darkness pressed against the window. Fredrik drew the curtains shut and gently rested a hand on Moa's damp shoulder. She looked at him as he traced a finger along her cheekbones, and her eyes fluttered shut.

He wanted nothing more than to shield her from the world's cruelty, but he knew he couldn't. He could barely save himself. He cursed himself for not bringing any decent nightwear; his old, faded gray boxers felt embarrassingly outdated.

"Wow, it's huge," Moa murmured, her eyes drawn to his shoulder.

She reached out to touch the scars—a cross of pink, puckered skin where the bullet had torn through him. The wounds had healed, but the pain lingered.

Moa fluffed his pillow, and as Fredrik's body sank into its softness, he sighed deeply.

"It still hurts," he admitted. "I'm not exactly a passionate lover."

Moa slipped an arm around his chest, resting her head against his neck.

This was the intimacy Fredrik had longed for all his adult life—simple and unburdened by complications. He moved closer to her, and they lay there silently, gazing at each other. Outside, the wind howled, and the lighthouse blinked steadily through a gap in the curtains.

"This is just the beginning," Moa whispered, drawing closer.

CHAPTER THIRTY-EIGHT
Nordby

The man instinctively clutched at his throat, gasping for air as panic surged through him.

Where the hell did the rope come from? He remembered a spray bottle aimed at his face. Someone calling himself Ziggy, with a reassuring smile, spoke in a familiar voice.

A second passed. Maybe two.

His final thought, before the darkness closed in, was the bitter realization that he had been deceived by someone he once trusted.

CHAPTER THIRTY-NINE
Wednesday, October 25

The night with Fredrik had done wonders for Moa's self-esteem, grounding her in a calm she hadn't felt in ages and injecting much-needed hope for the future. It was risky but worth it.

She had retrieved her duty weapon when Erik's voice, sharp with urgency, echoed through the corridor, accompanied by frantic radio chatter.

"Moa, thank God you're early. We need to go. Gather your things and meet me in the garage."

Erik's tense demeanor, the way he double-checked his weapon and holster, snapped her out of her romantic reverie.

Amid the stream of radio alerts, she caught disjointed words: eyes, beach, dog, patrols.

The seat in the van was freezing, and Erik navigated the morning rush with a steady hand, his focus razor-sharp.

"A man walking his dog found a pair of eyes at a rest area by the beach in Nordby," he said, his tone grim. "We're getting backup from another district to sweep the area all day if needed. Our first stop is to retrieve the eyes."

As the van's heater kicked in, warming the space, Moa braced herself for a long day. The radio crackled with reports of suspected drunk driving in Toft, a fight in an apartment, and then, barely a minute later, a call about a body found near a campsite in Nordby.

Erik's phone rang, and he answered in his commanding tone.

Moa stared out at the bleak landscape, lost in thought.

"Jan was out for a run and found the body," Erik said, breaking the silence.

"Jan? Where's the body?"

"Near a chapel in a small, wooded area close to the beach."

"I think I know the place."

"The eyes were found on a table by the beach," Erik added.

Two police cars were parked on the road near the chapel's parking lot, their blue lights switched off. The area around the chapel had been cordoned off, and thankfully, no curious onlookers had arrived yet.

A colleague approached them and reported, "The body is on the path by the large stone. We've kept our distance to avoid contamination. I think the face looks familiar."

"Good work, thank you," Moa replied, her voice steady. "Where's Jan?"

"He went to get his bag."

"Alright, we'll start at the beach first," she said, preparing herself for what was to come.

The cold air sliced through the warm interior of the bus as the window gap slowly sealed shut.

"I wouldn't be surprised if it starts snowing by the afternoon," Erik remarked, pulling the vehicle to a stop beside a patrol car.

A man with a brown dog spoke to two officers, his gestures and pointing making it clear he had come "from there" and walked "this way." The dog's long ears flapped in the brisk wind.

A narrow path led Moa and Erik down to the beach. Officers were scattered along the shore, one setting up a temporary cordon. To the right, about a hundred meters away, stood the luxurious Hotel Linden Oasis—its guests would soon find themselves once again being questioned by the police.

A pair of human eyes lay on a weather-beaten picnic table, their light blue irises staring directly at Moa. She felt a chill run down her spine.

Erik dropped his bag beside him. "For heaven's sake," he muttered, his voice tinged with disbelief.

Moa struggled to find the right words. "I don't even know what to say."

"We don't need to form any theories yet," Erik said, his tone steady. "Just document the scene. It's clear this is the work of someone seriously disturbed."

"Unfortunately, the killer seems to know what they're doing," Moa replied.

She started her recorder, carefully describing the findings and the location. They worked swiftly, recovering the almost intact eyes. No traces of blood could be seen on the table, benches, or surrounding ground.

"A K-9 unit is on the way," Erik noted. "Let's see what the chapel has in store for us."

Moa loaded their bags into the van as they prepared to move on. The site they were heading to had once been a church with an adjacent cemetery, offering final rest to sailors washed ashore. Only fragments of the foundation remained, with trees planted in a square pattern over the area where, in the seventeenth century, remains were discovered after a storm surge.

The police radio crackled in the background as the K-9 unit arrived, adding a sense of urgency to the tense atmosphere.

"I want you to expand the cordon," Erik instructed the patrol on-site. "There's a road running parallel to the campground—place a patrol there so no one can make their way down to the beach. We need three hundred meters secured in each direction."

As they approached the discovery site, a man's lifeless body came into view, lying on his back. The emergency services had already been there but realized they were too late and left. The path within the cordon was well-trodden, littered with scattered pinecones, dry grass, and overgrown heather.

The man's unbuttoned jacket revealed a white shirt beneath, his pants held up by a belt, and both shoes still firmly on his feet. His gray hair, streaked with mud, clung to the bald patches on his head. There were no apparent signs of head injuries, but the scene was unsettling.

A bird had been grotesquely stuffed into the man's mouth, with large parts of his face smeared in mud, likely from the puddles along the path.

"Holy shit," Erik muttered, turning his face away from the disturbing sight.

The man's eyes were missing—two empty sockets staring blankly.

Moa looked at the body, a spark of recognition flashing in her eyes.

"I think I know him," she said, trembling. "Isn't that Henning Hager?"

"The father of Jan?"

CHAPTER FORTY

Ziggy sat in his car, parked far from the cordoned-off area in Nordby. A sense of pride swelled within him as he examined his hands. Project Major Tom was unfolding precisely as planned. He had cleared the path. His emotions were dormant, and perhaps they had never been fully awakened.

Life always offered excuses; there was something or someone to blame.

He watched the police officers moving in different directions. Their adrenaline mirrored his own. The grand finale had played out flawlessly.

The cold seeping into the car nudged him to start the engine. With a mix of curiosity and confidence, Ziggy drove toward the barricade tape, ready to take a closer look at the chaos he had set in motion.

CHAPTER FORTY-ONE

Moa had cherished memories of the chapel, her first kiss among them. But now, those memories were replaced by the haunting image of a face without eyes. She noticed a deep groove on the man's neck, below his right ear.

"Here," she said, pointing. "He has likely been strangled with a rope. We'll conduct a body inspection until Jan arrives. Considering there was once a church here, this could easily be classified as a ritual murder. If it weren't for the recent murders and the bird in his mouth, that might've been true," she continued as she documented the scene. She moved to the path's edge, searching for details from a broader perspective. The man's clothing, the groove digging into his neck, and the bird in his mouth were the same species as the one found in Bernd's mouth and Rasmus's pocket.

Moa tried to reconstruct how the man had ended up there. She scanned the gravel for tire marks or signs of a struggle but found nothing. Methodically, she searched the path and saw only the remnants of a mushroom and a few sticks. The wind rustled through the coniferous trees, sending a low murmur through the grove.

In every graveyard, bodies rest alongside something less tangible—unfulfilled dreams, abandoned hopes, forgotten desires. The ground held more than remains; it was a final resting place for aspirations never fulfilled. The grand plans to change direction in life, the dream of a journey, the longing for a partner, and the hope to write a book were all buried with those who once carried them.

Moa switched off the recorder and returned to the body.

"No phone or wallet in his pockets," Erik said, double-checking the back pocket of the man's pants.

"What about the inner jacket pockets?"

"Empty."

A sleek black Audi pulled up, and Jan emerged, still dressed in his vibrant sportswear, now covered by a dark wool coat. He placed his bag on the ground and stood still, searching for the right words.

"As you might have guessed, it's my father, Henning Hager," he said, his voice steady but heavy.

"You can't—" Erik started but paused when Jan met his gaze, his expression firm and unyielding.

Moa snapped into autopilot. With no forensic pathologist nearby, they needed to move the body. They were racing against time while chasing evidence the wind snatched from their hands with every passing minute.

"Did you drive here this morning?" Moa asked, breaking the silence.

"I did. I parked on the far right. Photograph my tires and tracks before I leave—it'll save you time," said Jan and began documenting the scene. "Forensic technicians on the scene: Moa Bakke and Erik Storm. The body is that of a man in his seventies. Rigor mortis is fully developed. Signs of asphyxiation bleeding noted . . ."

Jan's voice was calm and deliberate, almost hypnotic. Moa found herself momentarily lost in its rhythm, struggling to focus on the task.

"My guess is someone returned to turn the body," Erik noted, his voice breaking through her thoughts. "The lividity on the back is less pronounced than on the front."

Jan gently adjusted Henning's shirt, his movements careful and deliberate.

"At the pat-down?" Jan asked.

"Neither wallet nor phone," Erik replied.

"The eyes we found down by the beach were in good condition. They couldn't have been on that table for twelve hours," Moa added. "I suspect they were stored in formalin before being placed there."

"As macabre as this is, it simplifies things that one of us found the body," Erik said.

"True. It would've been horrific if a child had stumbled upon this. It's unsettling, though, being both a witness, a forensic pathologist, and a relative. We'll see what the autopsy reveals tomorrow. I'm heading out—I need a shower and a change of clothes. See you at the station."

"My condolences," Moa said, listening to Jan's polite but hurried response as he made his way to the car.

"Surely, he's not planning to perform his father's autopsy?" Moa asked.

"No way. He's in shock. Jan handled himself well today, but he might need some time off. He looks worn out. Everything here is too clean. And that bird didn't fly into his mouth on its own. What on earth is happening? Can someone really hate both people and birds this much?"

They continued to comb through the area around the body, extending their search to the path, the forest grove, and the entire parking lot. Moa secured a pair of shoe prints in the gravel while Erik scanned for tire tracks.

* * *

A biting wind, heavy with salt, scraped against their faces as they wrapped up at the crime scene before one o'clock. The team from Falck carefully placed Henning into the gray bag. The sound of the bag being zipped up echoed, marking the end of the first phase of their investigation. In the distance, the sea's murmur grew into a thunderous roar.

As they prepared to leave the chapel, a solitary deer watched them from the edge of the trees, its gaze unblinking amidst the gathering storm.

CHAPTER FORTY-TWO

The breakfast area at Fredrik's hotel had taken on the atmosphere of a tense waiting room, where everyone held their breath, dreading the possibility of more bloodshed. The murders of Bernd and Rasmus still gripped the headlines, casting a shadow over the islands.

After Moa left that morning, Casper contacted Fredrik with good news: they would turn off the fan in the cottage during the day and patch up the wall. It gave Fredrik hope, reinforcing his decision to make a fresh start. Maybe it wasn't such a wild idea after all. The cottage appeared in his life like a sign, pushing him toward possibilities he hadn't considered before.

"Good morning," Hanna greeted him, interrupting his thoughts. She stopped by his table, cradling a steaming cup of tea. "Feels like we've experienced all four seasons this week."

"I haven't been outside yet, but it does feel like winter," Fredrik replied, pressing his palm against the cool glass.

His phone buzzed with a new message.

I know.

His heart skipped. Who was watching him? What did they want? Money? Or was it something more sinister?

The sound of Ingrid's heels clicking on the floor drew closer. Fredrik took a deliberate bite of his warm croissant, savoring the crispy layers. He spread a generous amount of bright red raspberry jam on the next piece, determined to enjoy the simple pleasures of being a tourist, for a bit longer.

The tranquility was short-lived. When he reached the corridor, he found Violeta standing outside his door, her eyes red and puffy. Fredrik had enough on his mind but couldn't ignore her distress.

"Sorry, I..."

She glanced nervously down the corridor. Fredrik hesitated, unsure what to do.

"I'm in a hurry, running an errand," he said.

Violeta looked down at her shoes, her fingers anxiously playing with the frills of her white apron.

"I need to apologize," she said, her voice trembling. She briefly met his gaze before lowering her eyes again. "I just... I needed to talk to someone."

A thought crossed Fredrik's mind. It was a long shot, but he hoped he was right.

"Are you the one who's been sending me messages?"

Violeta's eyes welled up with tears. For a moment, Fredrik nearly invited her in, but the past few days' events had sharpened his instincts. He kept his grip on the door handle, waiting for her to speak.

"No one would believe me," she whispered, her voice trembling.

The elevator doors slid open, and Ingrid stepped out, her expression as sour as ever. Fredrik flinched but quickly composed himself.

"Thanks, Violeta. I'll be back in the afternoon. Two pillows are enough," he said, his voice loud enough for Ingrid to hear.

Fredrik had planned a quiet morning with his book but found himself driving back to the lighthouse at Ylva's request. She needed to revisit the crime scene to clarify some witness statements.

The frantic energy from yesterday was gone when he pulled the handbrake. A sharp wind hinted at winter, keeping most visitors at bay. A few cars idled in the parking lot, and their occupants were content to view the lighthouse from afar. The press, having already captured their shots, were nowhere in sight.

"Thanks for coming on such short notice," Ylva said as Fredrik approached. "I spoke to Pia, the tour guide, yesterday and need to double-check everything with you again."

There was an edge to Ylva's tone that made Fredrik's heart race. He opened his mouth to respond, but she continued, "Can you show me exactly where you parked your car yesterday?"

Fredrik turned and pointed to the farthest corner of the lot. Ylva nodded and began walking toward it, with Fredrik following closely behind.

"Here?" she asked, stopping at the spot.

Fredrik demonstrated how he had parked, positioning the car to view the sea on one side and the lighthouse directly in front of him. Ylva paced back and forth, her brow furrowed.

"Did you plan to go up to the top of the lighthouse?"

"As I mentioned, I was driving around. It looked like it would rain, and I hadn't decided what to do," Fredrik replied, shaking his head to emphasize his point.

"The view is quite nice up there," Ylva remarked.

"I'm sure it is. I had considered going up to take some photos, but not yesterday."

Ylva pulled her scarf tighter against the wind, her demeanor cool and distant. "Can you fetch your car and park it like yesterday?"

Fredrik hesitated but complied. Ylva's previous warmth had vanished, replaced by a professional detachment. Once he had parked, she asked him to step out, then got into the driver's seat herself, snapping a few photos as Fredrik watched, a knot of unease tightening in his chest.

"The view of the lighthouse and the winding road leading to it is almost perfect, except for a few shrubs on the left that threatened to obscure the scene. But no, it looks fine."

Fredrik couldn't shake the unease gnawing at him.

It looked fine now, but what the hell hadn't been fine before?

"And Rasmus's car? It was parked where I am now, right?" Ylva asked as if trying to piece together a puzzle.

"Exactly, right by the information board."

"Stay in the car," Ylva instructed.

He watched as she started her ascent toward the lighthouse, occasionally glancing back at him. Tension tightened Fredrik's jaw.

With the lighthouse looming behind her, Ylva strolled back toward the parking lot, her phone in front of her.

Fredrik massaged his hands, feeling the creeping chill in the air. He recalled how he almost switched to becoming an undercover cop once. Long night shifts in freezing cars, sustained only by junk food and the promise of something more. He silently thanked himself for sticking to forensics and studying languages instead.

Fredrik stepped out of the car as Ylva approached, engrossed in her phone conversation. She shot him the occasional glance.

"I'll be off," she said, slipping her phone into her pocket. "We might need to run through this again. You know how it is."

"Of course," Fredrik replied.

"And you're staying until Sunday, right?" she asked.

"Yes. Do you need help interviewing the Germans at the hotel?"

Ylva shook her head, keys jangling as she pulled them out. "No. We've brought in a regular interpreter."

The air between them turned icy.

"Okay," Fredrik muttered, curiosity tugging at him, but he held back.

Ylva continued, "According to Pia, no cars were in the parking lot when she arrived. But she mentioned seeing a car like yours on the road behind the lighthouse. Then there's Max—he snapped a few photos of you."

Fredrik's heart raced, but he remained silent, knowing Pia's account was more crucial than Max's photos. After throwing Rasmus out of the lighthouse, Fredrik could have returned to his car. Theories raced through his mind.

Was there a road behind the lighthouse? Had they found tire tracks?

His phone buzzed in his pocket, pulling him back to the present. He waited until Ylva drove off before checking the message.

I know something. Must talk to you. Where can we meet?

Violeta! He had enough on his plate already. Besides, Violeta had been snooping around in his room. Would some incriminating evidence—like his old underwear— appear in the grass behind the lighthouse? He had to be prepared for anything. His finger hovered over Moa's contact, but he hesitated. Trust was a fragile thing now.

Was he a suspect in Rasmus's murder?

CHAPTER FORTY-THREE

A harsh glare from one of the overhead lamps in the station's meeting room stabbed Moa in the eyes. Squinting, she quickly switched seats, settling next to Erik. They had indulged in a greasy burger on their way back from Nordby—just the kind of carb-and-fat-loaded fuel that would keep them alert for a bit longer.

Erik and Ylva were eager to push the investigation forward, so they called for a brief, no-nonsense meeting. Anna, the prosecutor, was already there with a stack of papers neatly arranged in front of her.

"We'll make this quick," Erik began, his tone all business. "We still have a couple of forensic technicians out there, but so far, they've found little at the chapel. Ylva, why don't you start?"

"Absolutely," she said, leaning forward. "First, let's address the threats and our safety. We're on it, and everyone has our full support. If you feel even the slightest bit uneasy, report it immediately. We've also arranged for extra patrols to monitor the garage."

She flipped open a folder and continued, "Now, on to the report you sent me, Erik, regarding Bernd Jung. The feathers covering the body were a mix of goose down and goose feathers, treated with an antimicrobial substance—likely from a duvet or a pillow."

Erik exchanged a glance with Moa, who had the report in her stack. She had skimmed it earlier and could already picture herself combing through stores across the island in search of duvets and pillows in the coming days.

Ylva pressed on, "Bernd's phone was found in Rasmus's apartment, and the digital forensic team is digging into it. As you know, the USB drive was also recovered, and it turns out the two maps Fredrik saved were from that drive and are linked to Tim Klein. Fredrik did a good job photographing the drive. Both Tim's and Bernd's fingerprints were found on it."

Anna leaned forward and declared, "I decided to keep Tim in custody for as long as possible. His refusal to cooperate makes him particularly intriguing."

"He could be threatened, though," Moa interjected. "Maybe he knows something and feels he has to stay silent."

"Good point. We should consider that," Anna nodded.

Ylva, with a glimmer of interest in her eyes, added, "I took a closer look at the maps on the drive. There's a plan to build several holiday cottages around Nordby lighthouse in designated areas of the nature reserve and on part of the nearby golf course."

She let out a small, amused chuckle before continuing, "And it gets even better—there are plans to create artificial islands near Lynn Reef, which is also within the nature reserve. Whoever's behind this has quite the imagination. My guess? Someone from abroad, with a wild imagination and way too much money. You can sell a fantasy for a high price, and eager buyers and brokers are always ready to make a deal. As for Bernd Jung's death, the only logical explanation is that his devotion to nature got him killed. He was an obstacle. I'm looking into whether there's any truth to a potential wind farm expansion. Green Air is controlled by investors from Switzerland, with connections to stakeholders in the Middle East."

Ylva crossed something off her list, looked up and continued, "I also spoke to Fredrik again. The info I got from Pia doesn't line up with his statement. She says his car wasn't in the parking lot when she arrived at the lighthouse that morning. Do we have any updates on those tire tracks behind the lighthouse?"

"Nothing yet," Moa replied. "But there's a flood of new information coming in today; with any luck, we'll find a match on something soon."

Ylva said, "I've decided not to use Fredrik as an interpreter; it's better to bring in one of our own."

"Agreed," Anna replied. "Besides, he's here on vacation; no need to have him running around."

The words cut deep, but Moa kept her silence.

"I visited Hotel Linden Oasis near the chapel," Ylva continued. "I also had a couple of officers check for potential witnesses, but no one has seen or heard anything unusual in the past few days. The man who found the eyes was surprisingly calm and provided a clear statement. He's a former priest, and he described how his dog led him to the discovery. He walks the same route every morning and mentioned that he didn't notice anything unusual."

Ylva made a note on her paper and moved on. "Now, about the break-in in Nordby—it might seem minor, but everything points to Rasmus being involved. The place was tidy, and he covered his tracks well, leaving no evidence behind. The plastic sandals we found at the lighthouse match the shoe prints at the zoo. A similar pair, size forty-seven, was sold at Spar last Monday around midday. Unfortunately, it was a cash transaction."

Erik raised his head, and Anna quickly asked, "Surveillance footage?"

"We're waiting for it," Ylva responded. She paused, then added, "I've received word that Jan has been hospitalized. The initial diagnosis was food poisoning, but his fever is spiking rapidly. It could have been triggered by shock."

The meeting wrapped up, with Anna leaving the room looking displeased. Ylva and Erik got caught up in a conversation. Moa paid no attention to them as she was drained and had no energy left for a discussion she might be dragged into.

"Moa, can you take a look at this?" Ylva asked, holding out a surveillance photo.

"Isn't that the backyard of the luxury hotel in the city center?" Moa asked.

"Exactly," Ylva said. "I'm investigating a string of high-value car thefts—luxury cars worth millions are disappearing. This might be a witness."

Moa examined the photo and let out a chuckle. "That looks like me, but in a wig. I'm heading to The Vault for a coffee. Anyone want to join?"

The morning's tension eased, giving way to laughter.

CHAPTER FORTY-FOUR

The scent of geraniums wafted through the air as Fredrik approached the small medical station by the square, a subtle reminder of the tranquility around him. Moa had advised him to seek a second opinion. He needed reassurance, and Doctor Ulrik seemed like the rock Fredrik could lean on.

Ulrik listened intently as Fredrik detailed his injury, nodding thoughtfully.

"When was your last cortisone injection?" he finally asked.

Fredrik blinked. "I've never had one."

Ulrik raised an eyebrow but quickly masked his surprise.

"So far, only physiotherapy and gentle massage?"

Fredrik nodded again.

"No heat treatments? Ultrasound?" he probed.

"No," Fredrik said, his voice tinged with frustration.

He slowly peeled off his shirt, revealing the scarred shoulder that had been his constant companion in pain.

Ulrik gestured to Fredrik to grip his hands and squeeze.

"Not much strength there," Ulrik observed.

With practiced precision, Ulrik tested Fredrik's range of motion, his fingers tracing the scar with a methodical calm. He asked about Fredrik's lifestyle, diet, and any supplements or medications, piecing together the puzzle of his patient's condition.

"My daughter's a physiotherapist and osteopath. I'm sure we can help you regain your strength. Are you staying long?"

"I'm leaving Saturday but might return soon. I have a cottage here," Fredrik replied.

Ulrik nodded, already preparing the injection.

"I'll give you a cortisone shot now. Come back Friday for another. It's crucial to keep moving, but gently."

As the needle pierced Fredrik's shoulder, he couldn't shake the nagging thought that everything would eventually be okay. He left the clinic with a numb shoulder, a prescription for more potent painkillers, and a detailed medical certificate—just in case it became necessary to prove he hadn't been involved in Rasmus's murder.

His phone buzzed with a message from Nordsol: a car would arrive at five to empty the cottage.

The café in the small square, with chairs adorned with cozy blankets, looked inviting. Despite the gloomy clouds lingering over Fredrik's life, the sun shone, and he decided he deserved a treat. As he approached the entrance, he spotted Max standing there as if waiting for him.

"Hey, Max."

Max spun around; his untied shoelaces looked like an accident waiting to happen.

"Was gonna use the toilet," he mumbled, hesitating, turning back toward the café.

"Alone?" Fredrik asked, trying to read the boy's stiff posture.

Max didn't answer, his gaze fixed on the worn wooden floor.

"Hungry?" Fredrik tried again, glancing at the golden pastries behind the counter.

Max's eyes darted to the treats, but he quickly looked away, shoulders slumped. Sensing an opportunity, Fredrik leaned in.

"I was thinking of grabbing a snack. Want to join me? My treat."

Max turned slowly, his eyes betraying a flicker of interest. His jacket was surprisingly clean, and even his pants were free of the usual stains. But as he shuffled forward, he tripped over his laces, catching himself just in time. He glanced at a table near the patio heater.

"That's settled," Fredrik said, taking the lead.

Max carefully selected a pastry, his movements deliberate, as if the choice mattered more than satisfying hunger. For the first time, a glimmer of hope softened his usually guarded expression. Meanwhile, the pain in Fredrik's shoulder grew sharper with each pulse as the anesthesia mixed with the cortisone was starting to wear off.

Ulrik had assured him it would feel better by the afternoon, and Fredrik clung to that promise.

"Need help with those laces?" Fredrik offered, noticing Max's struggle.

Max shot him a glare, swinging his legs defiantly.

"I'm fine," he muttered, though his tone lacked conviction.

Without waiting for permission, Fredrik leaned over, double-knotted the laces, and handed Max a wet wipe. Max eyed it suspiciously.

"I'm clean."

"And I'm a forensic technician—I know how much dirt is everywhere. Trust me. Here."

Reluctantly, Max accepted the wipe, carefully cleaning his sticky hands. Fredrik took a large bite of his Friland pastry, the crispy vanilla layers giving way to a sweet burst of marzipan and strawberry jam.

"So, what's happening?" Fredrik asked, his voice a bit too casual, cringing inwardly at how awkward it sounded.

Max wiped his mouth with his jacket sleeve and sighed.

"Too many cops around."

"But things are starting to go back to normal now," Fredrik replied, trying to sound reassuring.

Max looked at him, then blew bubbles into his Fanta with a straw, clearly unconvinced.

"The guy on the beach this morning—do you call that normal?"

"What guy?" Fredrik asked.

Max leaned back in his chair, draping a gray blanket over his legs and crossing his arms defiantly. "You're a cop, aren't you?"

"I'm on vacation," Fredrik replied, dodging the question. "Want some more?"

Max shook his head, patting his stomach and pulling the blanket to his chin. Fredrik's mind drifted; he didn't have the energy to engage in an eight-year-old's wild tales. It was time to head back to the hotel.

"Dumb question, but aren't you supposed to be..." Fredrik started.

"At school?" Max cut in, mimicking Fredrik's tone with a smirk. "Maybe. Or maybe I got the day off. Who knows. Thanks for the snack, though. You're nicer than the other cops. I'm gonna talk to them later. But you know, it's dangerous to talk too much."

"I agree. But isn't having a criminal on the loose even more dangerous?"

Max shrugged, his expression indifferent, crumbs scattered around his mouth.

"I saw you," he said, leaning closer to the table, his voice dropping to a conspiratorial whisper.

Fredrik felt a surge of relief mixed with unease. How was he going to wrap this up? He hated the thought of leaving Max alone out in the cold.

"It was good you saw me," Fredrik said carefully. "Those photos you took really helped the police. Sometimes, people see different things, and the wrong person could get blamed. Photos—they're strong evidence."

Max nodded, finishing the last sip of his drink, his eyes meeting Fredrik's with a glint of something unspoken.

"Can you really catch a murderer with just a photo?" Max asked, his voice tinged with curiosity and doubt.

Fredrik considered his answer. "Yes and no. A photo can be compelling but becomes even stronger when combined with other evidence—DNA, shoe prints, fingerprints, or even a single hair left at the scene. In any investigation, a photo is one of the best pieces of evidence you can have."

Max's gaze drifted to the grocery store across the street. "Cameras are everywhere, so the murderer's probably been caught on one already."

"True," Fredrik nodded. "The key is—"

Max cut him off, his tone suddenly sharper. "But if you had a photo of the murderer, and he found out... you'd be in deep shit, right?"

Fredrik sighed inwardly, realizing he wasn't getting away from the conversation anytime soon. Max pulled out a white iPhone, glancing around before looking at Fredrik with a rare vulnerability.

"I'm scared," Max admitted, his voice barely a whisper.

Fredrik frowned. "Is that your phone? It doesn't look like the one you showed me yesterday."

"It's stolen. But don't tell anyone," Max muttered, his voice low. I had it yesterday."

As Max fell silent, an elderly couple shuffled to a table right before them. Despite the many empty spots in the café, Fredrik and Max found themselves in the shadows. Max waited until they were settled before he continued.

"There was an old man in the lighthouse yesterday. I took a photo of him."

Fredrik's mind raced, momentarily easing his suspicions about Pia's version of events. Still, he knew images could be easily manipulated—kids these days could handle image-editing apps like pros. He tried to calculate where Max could have taken a photo of the lighthouse.

"Did you see when..." Fredrik hesitated, catching himself. It wasn't right to interrogate Max like this. But then again, what did it matter now? He wasn't acting as a police officer, forensic technician, or anything official. He was a suspect, stuck in a web of questions. Children had wild imaginations, after all. Anything was possible.

Max ran his finger across the screen, pulling up the photo gallery. His eyes darted around, scanning for surveillance cameras before he placed the phone on the table. He zoomed in on an image—someone standing at the top of the lighthouse.

Fredrik's heart skipped a beat. He recognized him instantly.

CHAPTER FORTY-FIVE

Ziggy's hands had been a perfect fit around the slender neck. With each desperate demand, a dark force likely lurking within him his entire life surged to the surface. It spread through him like a demon, seizing control with a relentless grip. He didn't resist; instead, he surrendered to the overpowering wave, letting it take the lead.

This force was unstoppable, a guiding presence that knew precisely what to do.

Ziggy let himself be carried away by the tide of emotions and exhaustion. His body craved rest after days of relentless strain. He had intentionally overdosed, finding that it was the only way to keep functioning, to keep the noise in his head at bay. The trips cleared his mind, offering him a blank slate, a fresh start.

A new chapter awaited him, one where he would finally cash in on everything he'd been denied. He envisioned his future before him like a golden boardwalk, shimmering with good fortune.

Closing his eyes, he waited for the fire raging within to fade, hoping that when it did, he'd emerge from the flames and be reborn.

CHAPTER FORTY-SIX

It wasn't until Fredrik stepped back into the hotel that the realization hit him like a ton of bricks. How could he have been so blind? Max's words echoed relentlessly in his mind, sharp and accusing.

Ignoring the glaring warning on his medication—*avoid driving*—Fredrik hopped into the car. His heart pounded in his chest; each beat reminded him of the ticking clock. There was still time, but it was slipping through his fingers fast.

CHAPTER FORTY-SEVEN

Fredrik was jolted awake from his nap, the new painkillers having knocked him out cold. The shrill ringtone pierced the air—he needed to change it to something less annoying and ditch the vibration while he was at it. Better yet, he thought, why not turn off the phone entirely and shut out the world? He had completely forgotten that Nordsol was coming to the cottage to collect the old furniture, so getting up was inevitable.

Groggy and disoriented, Fredrik realized his arm muscles had become jelly during his brief slumber. Reaching for his phone, he accidentally knocked over a glass, shattering it on the floor. He cleared his throat, trying to gather himself as he struggled to rise.

"I need to have a word with you. Can you meet me in the lobby in half an hour?" Ylva's voice crackled through the phone.

"Sure, no problem," Fredrik replied, already knowing what was coming. He braced himself, pulling his aching body into a sitting position. The searing pain in his shoulder had dulled, his arm feeling more like his own again. Slowly, he tested its range of motion—outward, forward—it worked. He almost felt like a normal human being.

Outside the window, the pale light of dawn lingered, casting a cold hue over the room. He shivered, realizing he had slept for three hours—the first real rest he'd had all vacation. A daily siesta had been on his to-do list, but this was the first time he'd managed one.

Feeling unexpectedly refreshed and fully aware of the accusations Ylva had in store for him, he began to get ready. A message from Dennis popped up, saying he'd sorted out his bank issues and wished Fredrik a pleasant vacation. Dennis even mentioned he might visit Nordby someday; it certainly looked nice.

Fredrik ignored the Facebook notification icon. Among the messages was one from Irene. She missed him and urged him not to jump. He chuckled; autocorrect had gotten the better of her. Violeta had also reached out to discuss something. With all this swirling in his mind, Fredrik knew the day was far from over.

Fredrik stared at the scattered glass shards on the floor, deciding it was better to clean up the mess himself. The last thing he needed was the persistent maid poking around, so he ignored her message entirely.

There was a certain satisfaction in carefully crawling on the floor, picking up each shard without wincing in pain. After tidying up, he closed his suitcase. He secured it with a padlock—a temporary but effective deterrent for nosy amateurs who might be tempted to snoop through his belongings.

Back at the buffet table, Fredrik's eyes lit up at the sight of the remaining snacks and coffee. Without hesitation, he loaded up his plate with anything that looked delicious. His stomach, surprisingly cooperative, seemed to crave even more of the sugary treats and junk food.

The lobby was quiet, the construction noise finally silenced, and for the first time, he started to feel the relaxation of a true vacation. All that was missing was the warmth of a crackling fire.

Fredrik's mind raced as he systematically analyzed the photo on Max's phone—its implications, authenticity, and how best to respond. He had resolved to stay out of any further involvement. Yet, he couldn't help but wonder what accusations Ylva might throw his way and whether his tentative cooperation with the police was now a thing of the past. His best strategy was to stay one step ahead.

As he sat lost in thought, Ylva shattered his brief moment of peace, her glasses speckled with large raindrops. She invaded his quiet with a sense of urgency.

"There are a couple of questions I need to clarify with you," she said, her tone serious.

Fredrik was ready, armed with logical explanations and evidence. But the confrontation took an unexpected turn when Ylva pulled out her phone and showed him his Facebook profile.

"Maybe you can explain this?" she asked, her eyes locked onto his.

He stared at his profile picture—a snapshot of him smiling in the sunlight, taken by Dennis last summer. Ylva scrolled to the next image, revealing a brooding view from Hedborg's lighthouse under a dark, cloudy sky. Further down was his latest post, a serene photo of a lake at sunset, captured at the end of August.

A knot tightened in Fredrik's chest as he opened the photo from the lighthouse. The timestamp was glaring October 24, 10.03, marked with a cheerful smiley.

"Yesterday morning. Before Rasmus's death," Ylva said, her voice cold.

Fredrik's post had already gathered forty-three likes and a handful of comments. Worse, it was public—anyone could see it, not only his friends. Usually, he kept his posts within his tight circle, but this one had slipped through.

The silence in the lobby grew suffocating, wrapping around Fredrik like a noose.

One photo.

A damn photo with a smiley.

"What the hell is this?" he muttered, his prepared defenses crumbling like sand through his fingers. He looked up at Ylva, hoping desperately that her years of experience as a detective inspector would let her see the truth in his eyes.

"You know what this means," she said, her gaze piercing. "It could be used as potential evidence if it comes to that."

His only hope lay in the hands of an eight-year-old with a stolen iPhone. He knew the photo on his Facebook wasn't fake, but the one Max had shown him earlier still needed to be analyzed.

"What if I told you I haven't posted anything since August?" Fredrik cursed himself for not checking his account sooner.

"I'm surprised you haven't deleted the photo," Ylva replied, her skepticism palpable.

"I rarely check my profile," he said, his voice thin and unconvincing. "Honestly, I never do. I mostly read the news and ignore the notifications."

He unlocked his phone, hands trembling, and opened his Facebook account. The red notification icon displayed ninety-five alerts. He quickly took a screenshot of the post before deleting it.

"I don't know what to believe anymore," Ylva said, her eyes drifting toward the window.

Fredrik's hands trembled, stiffened by the shock of the situation. Slowly, he flexed his fingers, trying to regain control, and pulled out the certificate Ulrik had given him.

"It's not much," he began, his voice steadying, "but you know I'm incapable of throwing a man out of a lighthouse. I understand why you're suspicious, though."

He handed the certificate to Ylva, who glanced through it.

"Ulrik," she murmured, a hint of recognition in her voice. "I know him. I'll take a photo of this."

Fredrik noticed a softness in Ylva's tone, a subtle shift he knew he needed to capitalize on. As a former detective inspector, he understood the unspoken rules they both played by.

Fredrik scraped the last raspberry jam off his plate with a knife and licked it off, earning a disapproving look from Ylva.

"But, as I told you, I wasn't at the lighthouse yesterday morning. The last time I saw Rasmus was on Monday."

Ylva pulled out a notepad and jotted down single words, occasionally adding a question mark next to them.

"I didn't kill Rasmus," Fredrik stated firmly, locking eyes with her. He paused, then added, "But what happens if a child—say, an eight-year-old—finds a phone and doesn't hand it over to the police? A phone that might contain photos relevant to an investigation?"

Ylva looked up, her pen pausing on the page, giving Fredrik an approving nod.

"Who could have accessed your phone?" she asked. "Where have you left it unattended? Do you have any reminders with your passwords?"

Fredrik's mind raced as he replayed the last few days in his head, searching for any lapse in security.

"No notes. I've left the phone in my room a few times. The cleaning staff and Moa are the only ones who could've gotten to it. Maybe someone from maintenance with access to the room?"

"Do you use the open network here? Do you have a laptop with you?" Ylva asked, her line of questioning shifting gears, and Fredrik appreciated her problem-solving approach.

"I do have a laptop, but I don't usually log in on open networks—though maybe I did. Sometimes, I get paranoid and want to stop using social media. I have a password on the phone screen, and yes, I've used the laptop wirelessly."

Someone's been snooping in your room. Shouldn't you *mention* it?

Ylva seemed to sense his hesitation. "Of course," she said, "you're not a suspect. Not yet. But you understand there have been some strange coincidences. You would have reacted the same way. The prosecutor is under pressure to find a solution."

"I understand."

Ylva stood up, signaling the end of their conversation. "I need to get going. Is there anything else you can think of? An eight-year-old, you said? Found a phone? There won't be any punishment."

A temporary understanding seemed to melt the ice between them, but Fredrik knew his life was still on shaky ground. As he followed Ylva toward the door, the faces of Violeta and Moa loomed in his mind, each marked by the same big question marks that had yet to be answered.

CHAPTER FORTY-EIGHT

Moa steered her car toward Nordby, knowing this would be her last night at the hotel. The honeymoon phase was over, and she was ready to face reality and any new threats.

No matter how much she daydreamed of a perfect relationship, she knew it wouldn't work in the long run. Fredrik had his life in mainland Sweden, and he was still married. Moa wasn't about to waste more time waiting for idle promises to materialize. She'd been down that road before, and it had led nowhere.

They had agreed she would bring pizzas after her appointment at the hairdresser.

* * *

The salon, Cutting Crew, had been a fixture in Nordby for as long as Moa could remember, nestled near Café

Lykken. Nora, who ran the salon, was the mother of one of Moa's childhood friends from the summer holidays. Back then, Nora had tolerated the chaos of giggling girls demanding snacks and leaving seashells, sand, and sticks all over her carpet. Looking back, Moa realized how much stress they must have caused her.

As Nora's gentle fingers massaged Moa's scalp, she asked, "You've got a lot on your mind, haven't you?"

"That's putting it mildly."

"I don't know how you keep doing this job."

"Sometimes, I don't either. But someone must clean up the mess, right? And hopefully, put some of the dregs of society behind bars."

Moa's coffee sat untouched in front of her.

"How's the wig holding up?" Nora asked.

"It's fine. No one's noticed a thing. You picked a good one, thanks. Sometimes, it itches when I sweat, and I might take it off at the gym, but I must be prepared for the stares."

Nora caught Moa's smile in the mirror. "I see a few light strands at the back of your neck."

There was still some justice in the world, Moa thought, returning Nora's smile. She would have loved to close her eyes and drift off, avoiding the small talk altogether. Each chair in the salon was tucked into its little booth, offering a sense of privacy. Nora hadn't changed the decor since she opened the salon in the eighties; the soft pastel colors felt uplifting and welcoming.

"I'll apply a hair mask on the ends," Nora said. "There's quite a bit of saltwater in the wig."

"I've been out at sea," Moa explained. "My beanie was soaked when I got back. I haven't had time to wash it. I'd rather leave it with you."

Every trip to the hairdresser felt like stepping into a cloud of gossip and negativity, where small talk about illnesses and personal problems blended with the scent of hairspray. Moa often wondered how Nora could endure listening to people's confessions all day. Strangers bared their deepest secrets; at least crime scenes offered a quiet she preferred.

"Did the police drop by to ask any questions?"

"Not yet. But I've seen them drive by. Margunn and Geir at Lykken had a visit. They were asked a few questions."

With her robust frame, slender hands, and short nails always painted in dark polish, Nora moved with a practiced ease. For as long as Moa could remember, Nora had worn Chanel No. 5, a scent that Moa now associated with a carefree childhood. She watched Nora's movements, finally reaching for her cup. The coffee was weak enough not to upset her stomach but strong enough to keep her alert. Despite the gossip swirling around, the salon felt like a temporary refuge.

"Are you cold? Should I turn on the infrared heater?" Nora asked.

"Please do."

Nora rolled out the heating hood, surrounding Moa's head with warm, red threads that glowed like a grill. She placed a few magazines beside Moa's cup, a small gesture that made the salon feel even more like a safe haven.

"I went to an auction on Vidare Island this weekend," Nora began excitedly. "It was an estate full of old toys."

"Did you find anything new for your collection?"

"I did. Most people were there for the furniture, so I didn't have much competition. I got several beautiful dolls with handmade clothes."

"Do you dare to buy dolls at an auction?" Moa teased, shuddering at the thought.

Nora laughed, "You watch too much TV."

"Are you planning to sell them later?" Moa asked, still uneasy at the idea of bringing home a doll from an auction.

"That's the plan. I can't keep everything I find. My husband starts complaining."

Moa pulled out her phone and opened a photo of the music box she had received. "Do you know the value of something like this or where it might come from? It's a shame—it's missing its head."

Nora slipped on a pair of bright pink glasses and examined the image closely.

"A friend of mine started collecting music boxes," Moa lied smoothly. "When you lift the lid, it plays a lullaby."

"It's a shame it lost its head. If it were intact, it would be worth quite a bit. The wood appears walnut, likely made in Switzerland and custom-ordered by a Finnish furniture maker. Only about a hundred were ever produced, given away as Christmas gifts to loyal customers sometime in the sixties. I had one just like it, but I gave it away. Too bad—they're worth about two months' salary if they're in good condition."

As Nora spoke, Moa let her mind drift into the glossy pages of gossip magazines. She imagined the lives of the rich and famous—beautiful people sipping expensive wines on sun-drenched porches framed by clear blue skies. She drank her coffee, savoring the brief escape from reality.

Moa scheduled her next visit and accepted a small bottle of almond oil to soothe her scalp.

"Do you remember who you gave the music box to?" Moa asked as Nora slipped the bottle into a bag.

Nora paused, thinking back. "Oh, that was a long time ago. Let me see... yes, that young Austrian woman who was together with Jan. The one who disappeared. She was so sweet and helped me write some beautiful signs. If I recall correctly, she was pregnant at the time."

CHAPTER FORTY-NINE

After returning from the cottage, Fredrik collapsed onto the bed in his hotel room. The Nordsol staff had worked wonders, clearing out his run-down cottage, which now looked like a place with real potential. All that was left was to furnish the rooms. They advised him to leave the windows open for a few hours to clear the musty smell. Once they were gone, he checked his secret stash and pulled out a stack of bills.

Fredrik flipped through the channels, eventually muting the sound and reaching for his laptop. Irene hadn't contacted him, and he had no plans to share the money from selling the house—it was in his name, and he had paid for it in full.

He scrolled through his Facebook page; nothing new. To be thorough, he sifted through all his notifications. Thirteen hours ago, Jan had shared a YouTube clip of one of Fredrik's favorite songs, "Space Oddity." He clicked play, letting David Bowie's haunting, dry voice fill the room as he sang about Major Tom drifting into space.

Catching his reflection in the mirror opposite the bed, Fredrik saw a face that seemed to ask, *How the hell could I be so stupid?* The fact that Jan had shared a song about Major Tom, combined with the picture on Max's phone of Jan at the top of the lighthouse, was an intriguing connection he couldn't ignore.

Fredrik twisted on the bed, his body tensing as if bracing for an attack. Moa would be there any minute, and there were too many loose ends to make sense of. He needed to buy time.

Outside, the night was closing in, and the lighthouse's beacon cut through the darkness. It stood silently at the edge of the hill, guarding its secrets. Fredrik shuddered as an unsettling feeling gripped him. For the first time in a long while, he felt vulnerable. He hurried to draw the curtains, shutting out the eerie night, and tried to piece together the puzzle of recent events.

A knock on the door made him jump.

"It's me," Moa said.

Fredrik opened the door to find Moa with her hands full of pizza boxes. Her smile momentarily disrupted his logical thoughts, the aroma from the pizzas offering a brief escape from his spiraling mind. For now, he decided to stay in his bubble of temporary happiness, promising himself not to get involved in the investigation again—at least for a few more days.

"You look so much better," she said, placing the boxes on the tiny coffee table.

"You too," he replied, kissing her cheek and helping her out of her jacket. "I've been sleeping and lounging around all day. I could get used to this," Fredrik added with a grin.

"Did you see Ulrik?"

Fredrik lifted his arm and smiled. "Thanks to your recommendation, I'm a new man."

"I don't want a new man. I want you," she said, curling up in one of the armchairs.

They ate their pizzas, swapping slices and enjoying the food. But beneath the surface, a tense politeness hung in the air, like the fragile calm after an argument.

"I bumped into Ingrid," Moa said, breaking the silence. "She looked like she hadn't slept in days. Jan's in the hospital with acute food poisoning. His fever's rising, but he's strong—he'll pull through."

Fredrik absorbed her words, analyzing every detail without even realizing it. Moa continued, "I feel sorry for Ingrid. She looked so lost, so helpless. I guess anyone in a tough spot eventually gets worn down. Only a few can handle it."

"Yeah," Fredrik nodded. "They finally picked up the furniture, by the way. The cottage is empty."

"Great. So, are you planning to buy new things and rent it out?"

"As I mentioned, I'm going to return here soon, and I'll look for a job and get a start fresh. I'm putting the house up for sale. I meant what I said—my marriage has been over for a long time. You know how it is when you hit that point of no return."

"I know," Moa agreed softly. "I've got a few things to take care of tomorrow, so I'll sleep at home tonight. No more threats, thank God. We're hoping the situation is under control now. Need any help or advice on your shopping spree?"

"Absolutely. I'd love to have a beautiful assistant with an eye for home decor. We'll have to plan a housewarming party once everything's set up."

"You've already made friends here on the island."

Fredrik laughed and began scrolling through music clips. "Do you like David Bowie?" he asked.

"Not sure, I don't know his music. But by the way, that man with the dog you spoke to—he's the one who found the... well, he was down at the beach this morning."

"And?" Fredrik prompted, his attention shifting back to her.

"Haven't you heard about Henning?"

Fredrik's heart skipped a beat. Max had mentioned a guy on the beach earlier at the café, but Fredrik hadn't had a chance to check the news all day.

"I've been sleeping, ignorant to the world," he admitted. "The people from Nordsol mentioned all the drama here. It's become a standard phrase, so I just nodded along. What happened?"

"Henning was found dead this morning near the beach by the old chapel," Moa said, her voice dropping to a whisper. She pursed her lips, and Fredrik could tell she regretted saying anything.

"I'm sorry. I remember you mentioning him," Fredrik replied gently. "Maybe we should steer clear of work talk for a while?"

They settled onto the bed, and Fredrik found a music clip of a street artist in Stackaby. Moa moved closer, placing a hand on his leg. A man played the saxophone as people bustled in the background. It was sunny, with most passersby dressed in light summer clothes. Coins clinked into the saxophonist's open case while a sidewalk café appeared on the left. Some patrons sipped beer, their faces tilted toward the sun.

"Are you sleeping, Moa?" Fredrik asked softly.

"Not yet," she murmured. "I wish we were sitting in the sun, enjoying the peace. The saxophonist is really good."

"The sun will shine on us tomorrow on our day trip to Vidare Island," Fredrik began, but something on the screen caught his eye. In the café, a tall, well-dressed man removed his sunglasses to glance at the menu. Across from him, a woman slid her hand under the table, resting it on his leg. The saxophonist played on as more coins filled his case.

"Look there!" Fredrik said, pausing the clip and pointing.

"Good Lord. That's Jan and the woman from the lighthouse—what was her name? When was this recorded?"

Fredrik leaned forward, squinting at the details. "The clip was uploaded over the summer. It has seven hundred and eight views. Her name is Pia."

"Save it. Take a screenshot. Send me the link," Moa said urgently, grabbing her phone.

The clip, along with Max's photo, could be the key to clearing Fredrik's name and unraveling a web of murders.

CHAPTER FIFTY
Thursday, October 26

It was Fredrik's fifth day at the hotel. Ylva and Erik had received the screenshot and the YouTube link featuring Jan and Pia. The hotel was eerily quiet, as if wrapped in a cocoon. There was no sign of Hanna or Ingrid; the only hint that the staff was still around was the faint aroma wafting from the buffet. Outside, the landscape was serene; even the usually noisy construction site next door had gone silent. The only sound breaking the stillness was the clink of Fredrik's cup against the saucer. For a brief moment, he felt old, as if this was a preview of a retirement home.

The sudden rumble of a car engine approaching interrupted his thoughts. Doors slammed, and Ylva appeared, striding purposefully toward his table. Instinctively, Fredrik stood up, hesitating before deciding to sit back down.

"We need to talk," she said, her voice firm as she discreetly flashed a search warrant for his room.

Her expression made it clear—Fredrik was in trouble. Again. He gathered his cup and sticky pastry, retreating to his room with a sense of foreboding. As the door clicked shut behind them, Ylva handed him a series of photos taken from a surveillance camera in a store.

"I'm not sure what to make of this," she said; cold professionalism replaced the previous day's understanding.

"The images are from the Spar grocery store. On Monday, you purchased a pair of orange sandals—the same sandals found in the trash at the lighthouse when Rasmus was discovered. Our image team also confirmed that the photo posted on your Facebook page is authentic. There are too many inconsistencies, Fredrik. If you cooperate, things will proceed more smoothly. I must search your hotel room, bags, car, and cottage."

Fredrik took a slow sip of his coffee, using the moment to take a bite of his pastry. A rebellious surge ran through him. Part of him wanted to tell Ylva to go to hell and throw her out of the room.

"No problem at all. I'll unlock the bag," Fredrik said calmly.

Ylva nodded and got to work, looking oddly out of place in a poorly fitting uniform—so different from the sharp, tailored outfits he'd seen her in before.

"I need to open these," she said, placing three wrapped packages on the bed.

Fredrik shrugged, trying to mimic Max's practiced indifference. Ylva quickly unwrapped the packages, revealing three pairs of plastic sandals. She glanced at Fredrik, surprise flickering in her eyes, while he sipped his coffee, staying true to his promise not to interfere. She examined the size of the orange sandals while Fredrik watched with quiet anticipation, curious to see how things would unfold.

A knock at the door interrupted them. Ylva opened it to reveal Violeta, her face streaked with tears. The moment she spotted Fredrik, she pointed an accusatory finger at him.

"I've tried to tell him. I can't take it anymore," she said, her voice trembling as she pulled out a tissue to wipe her nose. Ylva, sensing the urgency, allowed Violeta inside even though she wasn't on duty.

"What happened?" Ylva asked, turning to Violeta.

Violeta stepped forward; her voice strained. "I've been fired—my husband too, so it doesn't matter now. Jan is in the hospital, so he can't come after me. Many things have gone missing here, and everything has been chaotic since they opened. I didn't dare say anything because I'm only a cleaner. The other officer who was here took no notice of me."

"You mean Rasmus Iversen?" Ylva asked.

Violeta's eyes filled with tears, and she nodded. "And him," she added, pointing at Fredrik. "He didn't respond to my messages. I thought maybe he could help."

"What exactly has disappeared?" Ylva asked, her tone darkening as she adopted a more authoritative stance.

"I was the only cleaner, so I managed the storage room. New duvets and pillows went missing. I was afraid they'd blame me. Then I read about what happened to the German man and the thing with the feathers, so I thought maybe it was all connected."

"Here's what we'll do," Ylva said, motioning toward the door. "Wait at the reception. I'll be down in a few minutes, and you can tell us everything. I want to hear your full story. I really do."

Violeta shot one last glare at Fredrik before leaving the room.

"This investigation is going to go down in history," Ylva muttered, placing the photos back in her folder. "I'm so sorry, Fredrik. I spoke with Max yesterday. He handed over the phone, said he found it, and we chose to believe him. The image analysis team confirmed the photo on Max's phone is authentic. Jan's in the hospital with a high fever, so I can't question him now. Again, I'm sorry."

Ylva extended her hand, and Fredrik shook it firmly.

"If it were my investigation, I might have done the same," Fredrik admitted. "There are so many scattered pieces, and a lot has happened."

He held back from asking the burning questions. But he couldn't help wondering about Jan's motive for killing Rasmus, and whether Jan was also involved in Bernd's murder. Still, it was hard to believe that Jan had killed his father and tried to set up Fredrik by accessing his laptop.

"I'll go talk to Violeta. She seems to have a lot to say. I understand why you didn't want to get involved. It's a shame it had to come to this. I'm truly sorry."

Her apologies kept coming, but Fredrik could tell they were genuine.

"I wasn't exactly eager to dig through your things or your trash," she added, giving the wastepaper basket a light tap with her foot.

"That's it!" Fredrik suddenly exclaimed, his eyes widening as he stared at it.

Flashes of that first interview, where he had served as an interpreter, flooded back. Ylva paused, releasing the door handle as she turned back to face him. Fredrik met her curious gaze.

"The wastepaper basket, damn it. Rasmus clipped his nails over the basket. And Jan was in the room."

Fredrik's breath quickened, his words tumbling out in a rush.

"The basket must have stayed in the room after we left. Rasmus's DNA was sitting there, waiting to be collected."

"I can cross-check the timing in the documentation," Ylva suggested.

"Here," Fredrik said, fishing the tag from the duvet. "I took a picture of the tag. I liked the bedding and the pillow, so I figured I'd buy the same. Now, after all this, I might reconsider."

Ylva studied the tag, her expression thoughtful as she snapped a photo.

"I'll talk to Erik," she said. "We'll send forensic technicians to comb through the linen closet if needed."

"I'm leaving now," Ylva added, her voice softening. "I'll take Violeta to the station. I'll be in touch. Thank you, and I'm truly sorry."

* * *

Fredrik had pieced together a crucial realization thanks to Max's probing questions. If Rasmus hadn't been found dead, the sandals might never have come to light. Fredrik had been too exhausted when he bought them and hadn't thought twice about tossing them away. But once back at the hotel, a plan began to form. He decided to find identical sandals, knowing they could be key. He scoured a few small kiosks without surveillance cameras and found precisely what he sought. Nearby, a tiny stationery store sold gift paper. He bought orange sandals in size forty-seven for his dad, blue in size thirty-eight for his mom, and a pair of red in size forty-two for the neighbor. The idea that he might be suspected of murder never crossed his mind—when he was planning a break-in at the zoo.

CHAPTER FIFTY-ONE

Fredrik found comfort in the simplicity of the yellow fields and flat landscape they passed through. The minimalism resonated with his plan to furnish the cottage with only the essentials—a fresh start with no clutter. He intended to secure his money in a new hiding place later that evening.

As Moa turned onto the highway, the island's landscapes seemed to brace themselves for the impending cold months. She declined an incoming call.

"Erik again," she said, a hint of exasperation in her voice. "I'll call him back when we reach the port in Stackaby. How's your shoulder?"

"I've forgotten to check—probably a good sign that it's much better. What's your take on Jan?"

"Honestly, anything's possible at this point. I think we've started to uncover what's going on. And if Pia, the tour guide, lied in her testimony, she's in deep trouble. She played her part well. Also, it was probably Jan who sent the music box. But here we go, talking about work again. I was supposed to be your guide today, and I need to unwind on my day off. The Friland Islands have more to offer than murder mysteries."

"It's hard to avoid discussing work, but we can try."

Moa alternated between being a stressed forensic technician and an enthusiastic tour guide. Fredrik thought she would have made an excellent guide, as she genuinely cared about the islands and their history.

Without prompting, she continued, "About ninety thousand people live on Vidare Island. Tourists often come for day trips to spot seals, enjoy a crab lunch, or go oyster picking. There's even organized bunker tours on Vidare."

"Bunker tours?" Fredrik laughed, imagining a group of history buffs who could name every general from every war.

"Yep," Moa said with a grin. "There are about two hundred bunkers on the Friland Islands, built by the Germans at the start of World War II. Friland was occupied quickly, as you probably know."

Once again, she revealed her depth. History and geography fascinated her, and Fredrik wished he'd paid more attention to those subjects in school. He pretended to keep up, but much of it had faded from his memory over time. The road stretched straight and flat before them. Fredrik searched his mind for something to talk about besides the case. Their time together had been a whirlwind of work-related events, and he was eager to experience Vidare with fresh eyes, this time as a tourist.

"And what about the other islands, like Breda?" he asked.

"Breda is where the wealthy retreat when they want to indulge," Moa explained. "Many people who work at the oil terminal on Fossa Island or the oil platforms in the North Sea, come to Breda to unwind. The hotels and restaurants there are top-notch—no campsites or fast-food chains in sight. There are rumors that international celebrities and business tycoons have built multi-million-dollar villas on Breda.

As they approached a community, the trees, bushes, and houses lining the road brought Fredrik back to reality.

"It's a peaceful drive up here," she said as if reading his thoughts. "I heard you decided to introduce the FLO method with family liaison officers?"

"That's right," Fredrik nodded. "The method aims to break the culture of silence and take some pressure off the lead investigator after shootings."

It was impossible to talk about oysters and campsites.

"Our shooting statistics are low, but that could change quickly. We're starting to attract young digital nomads and offshore companies to the islands. We expect to deal with increased fraud and money laundering soon."

They passed a smokehouse with an old, weathered fishing boat on display outside. They arrived at the ferry port after a stretch with warehouses on one side and the sparkling sea on the other.

"It takes about an hour to get to Vidare," she said. "If the wind picks up, it might take longer."

Passengers gathered at the terminal, stretching their legs while seagulls circled overhead, screeching as they searched for scraps. One gull made a daring dive into the sea, its cry piercing the air.

"I used to go to Vidare with my mom when I was younger," Moa reminisced. "Just for day trips. We always talked about staying overnight at a cozy hotel but never got around to it. Time slips by so fast."

"Exactly," Fredrik agreed. "We rush through life, and only when we hit a wall do we stop to wonder what happened to all those plans we made and all the dreams we never lived."

"I've been running my whole life," she confessed. "Filled my house with things, packed my schedule with activities and events. But in the end, I felt empty—like ticking off time. My best decision was to leave the house, all the stuff, and Glenn behind. I packed a few boxes of personal things and started over."

As Moa returned Erik's call, his voice crackled from the speaker. In the distance, Fredrik spotted the bow of the approaching ferry slicing through the water. The waves lapped gently at the dock, promising a calm, relaxing day—their first travel memory together.

Moa's expression shifted. "We have to turn back," she said, her voice tinged with regret. "The case has taken a serious turn."

CHAPTER FIFTY-TWO

Ziggy had dabbled with LSD a few times but quickly realized it wasn't for him. The chaotic swirl of sensations and the loss of control brought him no peace. He preferred the deep, heavy relaxation opiates offered, where blurry images and colors melded together behind his closed eyes. But now, something felt different. What the hell had he taken?

A needle punctured his vein, and voices erupted around him. Someone was shouting his name, accusing him of something, while another voice reassured him everything would be fine.

Horrified faces loomed above him, their twisted expressions seared into his mind. When their bloody skin brushed against his, electric shocks jolted through his body. A scream cut through the chaos, and then he saw them—the eyes without a face, staring into his soul.

A woman raised her hand, and Ziggy instinctively tried to block her, but his body refused to move. The fire raging inside him had melted his bones, leaving him paralyzed, reduced to stumps. Her long, red-painted nails raked across his cheeks, turning his screams into helpless, mocking laughter. Rivers of boiling blood poured down his face, searing his skin.

The colors that once swirled around him began to shrink, pixelating into tiny dots as a crushing weight pressed against his chest. Each breath became a struggle, the mocking laughter growing louder as the light and colors vanished, leaving him trapped in suffocating darkness.

CHAPTER FIFTY-THREE

Due to the change in plans, Fredrik had the rest of the day at his disposal. He still hadn't read a page of the book whose title he couldn't remember. He spent the day hunting for furniture. The idea of staying on the islands and skipping the trip home seemed more appealing by the minute.

Something felt odd as he approached the hotel. The parking lot was swarming with police cars, both marked and unmarked. A uniformed officer stepped forward as Fredrik pulled in.

"I'm a guest at the hotel," he said, flashing his interpreter badge to confirm his identity.

"One moment, please," the officer replied, his voice rough and raspy, his skin weathered. He reached for his radio while other officers strung barricade tape around the lot. Fredrik's name crackled over the radio.

"You're clear to enter. We're evacuating the hotel."

At the entrance, a flurry of activity caught Fredrik's eye—Hanna, frantically gesturing toward the new wing of the building.

"Speak with the woman at the entrance—Hanna, I think. She'll give you instructions."

"Thanks, I know her."

Hanna spotted him when he stepped out of the car, her face a mix of despair and barely held-back tears.

"I was about to call you. The hotel is shutting down. I've arranged a room for you at Hotel Linden Oasis. Pack your bags and leave immediately."

Her urgency left no room for small talk. Plain-clothes officers moved through the reception, speaking in low tones into their phones. Fredrik hurried to his room, gathering his belongings in less than five minutes. As he cast a final look around the room, a pang of sadness hit him—despite everything, he would miss the place.

* * *

The receptionist at the other hotel was a young woman with rosy cheeks and a smile so infectious it could brighten anyone's day. Yet, beneath her professional demeanor, there was a flicker of sympathy as she handed Fredrik his key.

His new accommodation—a luxurious beach villa with floor-to-ceiling windows—perfectly reflected the simple Nordic style he envisioned for his cottage. The terrace boasted a hot tub overlooking the sea, inviting relaxation. Curious, Fredrik explored the space, opening kitchen cabinets with enough provisions to cook for a small gathering. Upstairs, two bedrooms offered a stunning, calming ocean view through a massive window. In the living room, three logs were perfectly set in the fireplace, waiting for the spark to turn a sunny day into a cozy, rainy afternoon—the setting Fredrik dreamed of for enjoying a cup of tea by the fire. His mind buzzed with creativity and ideas and solutions for his new lifestyle.

He needed to collect the remaining money from the cottage and hopped into the car.

As he drew closer, a chill crept up his arms, raising goosebumps. A dog's sudden bark broke the uneasy silence. His heart sank as he spotted four patrol cars parked outside. It was too late to turn back.

CHAPTER FIFTY-FOUR

Moa sat quietly in Erik's office, waiting for him to finish his telephone conversation.

"What's happened?

"Moa, I'm glad you're here. I can always count on you," Erik began, his voice steady but tense. "Jan is unconscious—he's battling histoplasmosis and E. coli, suffering from seizures, high fever, and severe breathing difficulties. We can't communicate with him, but he's the prime suspect in Rasmus's murder. A patrol is stationed at his hotel, and the Environmental Protection Agency has sealed it off until we can rule out contamination. Ingrid mentioned that Jan had stayed at his summer cottage for the past few nights. They found bird droppings in the well water."

Erik picked up his notepad and continued, "We got confirmation that the tire tracks we found behind the lighthouse on Tuesday morning match Jan's Audi. The feathers covering Bernd might have come from Jan's hotel—our team is checking that now. Fredrik spoke with Ylva and pointed out something odd. Rasmus was seen clipping his fingernails into a wastepaper basket while they were interviewing hotel guests. During Bernd's second autopsy, no traces of Rasmus's DNA were found under Bernd's nails. It's possible Jan saved those nail clippings to use against Rasmus. The motive is still unclear, but Fredrik did an excellent job catching that detail."

Moa absorbed the gravity of the situation.

"This morning, there was a shooting in Byrum," he continued. "An industrial building turned out to be a hideout for a gang dealing in stolen electronics. There are at least four dead and a dozen injured. We're stretched thin, as usual."

Footsteps echoed in the corridor, mingling with the relentless chatter on the police radio. Erik's inbox pinged incessantly, filling with emails demanding his attention.

"Let's get to it," Moa said, her determination clear. "I'll change into my uniform."

Moa had countless questions, but her primary focus was finding evidence. It was Ylva and Anna's job to piece it all together.

"Ylva mentioned that the hotel cleaner clearly stated she didn't need to clean the room Rasmus used during the interviews. She said no one had touched the wastepaper basket—she checked. Ingrid was extremely meticulous about details. Even a single piece of gum meant changing the bag, so Fredrik's observation was vital."

Moa instinctively straightened her back at the mention of Fredrik's keen eye.

"I remember Rasmus's habit of constantly trimming his nails," she added. "He even did it a few times in my office. It seemed like a nervous tick."

Erik's tone grew more serious. "We need to comb the hotel and find anything that links Jan to Rasmus's murder. There are still many unanswered questions about Bernd's death. According to Ylva, Jan has the financial resources and connections to arrange something as elaborate as a helicopter. We must search his house, summer cottage, car, and office."

Erik stood up, tearing a page from his notepad. "I'll meet you in the parking lot in five minutes. We'll start at the cottage."

* * *

Fredrik's car came into view as their van rumbled down the gravel road.

"He seems to pop up everywhere. Strange," Erik said, slowing down.

"Not really," Moa replied. "The cottage on the right belongs to him."

Erik chuckled. "If he's looking for a vacation, he should probably head home."

They shared a brief laugh, easing the tension. But Fredrik's expression darkened as a patrol moved to block his path.

"It's okay," Erik called out. "Let him through and set up a cordon at the turning point. He's seen more than enough of us lately."

Fredrik gave a brief wave and disappeared onto his property.

"After this morning's search of his room, he probably wants us to keep our distance," Erik mused.

Moa nodded, pretending to understand the full scope of the situation. She knew she could catch up on the details later.

CHAPTER FIFTY-FIVE

Fredrik could almost hear his heart pounding in the silence of the empty cottage. He slipped into one of the bedrooms, staying out of sight from the window facing Jan's property. The lingering smell of fresh paint hung in the air. Though the police weren't after him, a nagging sense of guilt urged him to grab the money and get out as quickly as possible.

Two police officers strung barricade tape between the trees near Fredrik's fence. He had done this a thousand times, watching as curious onlookers gathered, hungry for excitement in their mundane lives. The thought crossed his mind—was life so dull that people needed a uniformed officer with plastic tape to make it exciting? He quickly retreated to the living room.

Outside, the unkempt grass and a few scraggly trees offered little cover. Glancing over his shoulder to ensure he was still alone; Fredrik began moving the stones. This time, they didn't seem as heavy. After shifting the tenth stone, a plastic container appeared, which he swiftly stashed in a bag. In the second pile, he uncovered another container.

Fredrik kept rearranging the stones, spreading them out to cover his tracks. He had rehearsed an excuse about spotting a badger behind the cottage if anyone asked.

He divided the banknotes into three bags, hiding two smaller bundles under the sink and pocketing the thickest one.

A patrol car blocked the exit as he headed out, sending his nerves into overdrive. Zipping up his jacket, Fredrik looked around, trying to steady his racing pulse. An officer glanced in his direction from behind the trees. Fredrik cleared his throat and jingled his keys, counting slowly to ten as he tried to regain control.

"Excuse me, you're blocking the way. I need to leave," he called out.

His hands trembled on the steering wheel as he drove toward Toft while the fog was rolling in and blurring the sea. The dense pine forest flanking the road offered a false sense of security, and his mind raced.

Once he got home, he resolved to tackle the to-do list he had been avoiding. It was time to sort out his life once and for all. He would hire a removal firm to collect anything worth selling; the rest would go straight into the trash. His father had already contacted a real estate agent who had found potential buyers. Fredrik had also contemplated selling his modest art collection to boost his pension fund.

His father rang, and his voice was breathless and frantic.

"It's on fire! Can you hear me? Hello?"

"Where's the fire? At your place?"

"Your house is on fire. Irene called. The fire brigade is on their way. Damn it, she took the car and left. Didn't want to come here. She sounded odd. Your mom and I are heading over to see if we can do anything."

CHAPTER FIFTY-SIX

The cottage looked almost as Moa remembered. Erik steered the car through the gate and parked between two spindly pines. A patrol stood by the well, their expressions a mix of curiosity and unease.

"By chance, we found this well covered. It was completely overgrown with weeds. What do you think?" an officer asked.

Moa crouched down, shining her flashlight into the dark, roughly three-meter-deep well. A skull emerged from the shadows, partially hidden behind a thigh bone.

"Maybe we've found Jan's girlfriend—the woman who vanished," Moa speculated, glancing up at Erik.

"I heard from Ylva," Erik replied. "She left the hotel and went to the hospital to speak with Ingrid. She'll head over here as soon as she's done."

Moa braced herself, mentally preparing to face yet another crime scene.

"Let's get to work," Erik said, unloading the equipment. "Moa, I need you to take photos. I'll document the findings."

The efficient, no-nonsense Erik she had known from their early days at the station was back in full force—a relief under the circumstances. Phones buzzed, and the on-site patrol dispersed to their following tasks.

"We'll need help from the fire department to retrieve the remains," Erik added.

Moa knelt, snapping several photos of the bones. The skull was remarkably well-preserved, and she could tell from the shape of the eye sockets and the absence of pronounced brow ridges that it was of a woman.

"The fire department will get here as soon as they can," Erik continued, "but they're tied up with a large fire at a gym in Toft. The smoke is intense, and nearby residents are being evacuated. We'll have to wait before sending in a forensic pathologist and anthropologist until we can recover all the remains."

The forensic anthropologist, stationed on another island, would need at least two hours to arrive. It was already late afternoon.

"One of the bathroom cabinets is locked," reported an officer. "We were about to open it when we got sidetracked by the well discovery. Oh, and we found a bunch of small birds in the freezer."

"We need to secure everything inside the house," Erik said firmly. "We don't yet know exactly what we're looking for, but it's possible Jan used this cottage as a meeting place. Anything could be relevant. Ingrid mentioned that the cottage hadn't been lived in for years, but Jan had stayed here for the last few days. She also said his behavior had become increasingly erratic, and the arguments were escalating."

At one time, the plot had been graced with lush, vibrant grass, the kind that once made Jan's cottage the epitome of summer life. Moa and her friends used to take the shortcut along the path beside the cottage, eager to reach the main road and the candy store. Back then, Jan's place was always buzzing with life—towels draped over the drying rack, the air filled with laughter, music, and the hum of summer parties.

Now, as Moa stood there, she couldn't help but feel a pang of loss. Her dreams of owning a beautiful house like this, filled with lanterns and well-dressed friends, were now tainted. Those innocent aspirations had fueled her drive for so long, but the scene before her was a stark reminder of how easily life could spiral out of control. Her house could have been under investigation if she had taken one wrong step. Once so clear, the thin line between right and wrong seemed dangerously blurred. She knew there were forces she couldn't fight and people who wished her harm. Yet, she also needed to trust someone—but given everything that had happened in the last few days, how could she?

Jan's cottage was a picture of carefully curated designer furniture and stylish items perfectly placed as if from a magazine. A narrow hallway guided them into the living room, where a wicker seating arrangement sat invitingly. But beneath this facade of luxury, sooty traces of black powder hinted at something far darker lurking beneath the surface. Erik moved toward the bathroom, where the wooden door groaned and resisted, refusing to open fully. Dark moisture stains marred the once-white ceiling. He opened the wall cabinet, and the musty mold odor filled the room immediately. A small white cabinet was partially concealed behind a row of deodorants and soaps. Erik deftly picked the lock, and his eyes widened.

"Well, this is interesting."

Neatly organized pill packets lined the right side, while bags of white powder and several small containers of clear liquid occupied the center. A box of injection needles stood upright among the stashes. Erik began pulling out the suspected drugs one by one. A blue-and-white toiletry bag rustled at the back of the cabinet as he unzipped it. Inside, he found beauty products long past their expiration date—by eight years.

"A toothbrush," he said, holding it up.

"Let's hope it matches the DNA from the femur in the well," Moa replied, her voice steady. "We need to close this tragic chapter."

She turned to grab a few more evidence bags and checked the time. The police radio crackled to life, requesting another car to help cordon off the fire scene and keep curious onlookers at bay. Sports Academy, the largest gym in Toft, was engulfed in flames. Erik said, "Ylva called. Jan died about fifteen minutes ago."

Moa froze. The word "karma" echoed in her mind. She used to laugh at such ideas, but who knows? Her mother's words: "Evil seed, evil harvest," made sense. Perhaps the birds had finally exacted their revenge in Jan.

"I don't know what to say," she murmured, her gaze drifting to the well.

Erik said, "A patrol will stay here overnight, and the area will remain sealed off. I'll request more staff so we can continue tomorrow."

* * *

By ten o'clock, Moa was stretched out on the sofa, exhaustion settling in. Fredrik had received a brief message saying they'd be in touch the following day. He replied with a simple thumbs up, which scored him points with Moa. She couldn't stand clingy, insecure men who bombarded her with questions. As always, it was her logic that kept her focused.

The bones found in the well had been preliminarily examined, and it was likely they belonged to Gisela Rebsdorf, Jan's young girlfriend, who had mysteriously disappeared before reaching her destination. In addition, fifteen small birds were discovered in the freezer. The team had worked swiftly, but with each grim finding, the chatter had died down, replaced by a heavy, uncomfortable silence.

Everyone had slipped into a mental autopilot, perhaps silently blaming themselves for not noticing any signs of Jan's darker side. They all wondered how someone so vile could hide behind such a perfect facade.

CHAPTER FIFTY-SEVEN
Friday, October 27

Fredrik stepped into the breakfast room at Hotel Linden Oasis. The brick floor complemented the rustic decor while a welcoming fire crackled in the fireplace. An energetic waitress with braids greeted him with a warm smile.

"There is freshly baked bread on the sideboard," she said, gesturing toward the inviting spread.

Moa's message from the previous night had been brief. Given the flurry around Jan's cottage, Fredrik knew she'd be tied up for the rest of the day. He missed hearing her voice.

Relieved, Fredrik indulged in a few extra days at the hotel until the cottage was ready.

With a clean set of clothes and his laptop, he was ready to start fresh once he returned to mainland Sweden to tie up all loose ends.

His father had confirmed the worst: the house was destroyed, along with Fredrik's car, which had been consumed by flames in the garage. The fire brigade was still on the scene, and Fredrik was waiting to hear from the insurance company.

Finally, a message from Moa appeared on his phone.

Good morning. I'm free after the morning meeting. I have lots to tell. Will call you later. xx

Fredrik helped himself to coffee, juice, and a plate of food. As he bit into a slice of rye bread, his phone buzzed.

A man with a dry, deliberate voice from the insurance company informed him that the fire was likely arson, pausing with a deep breath before each sentence.

"There will be a thorough investigation. We expect your full cooperation in this matter. And it will take time."

Fredrik mentally listed the few positives in his life and built a wall around himself, determined to take things one day at a time.

CHAPTER FIFTY-EIGHT

The meeting at the forensic department kicked off at eight o'clock. Moa was eager to be there, knowing she'd be off until Monday and wanting to stay in the loop.

Erik stood at the head of the table, his presence commanding respect and exuding calm authority. Moa stretched, trying to shake off the lingering fatigue. Erik stepped forward as the room settled, and the scraping of chairs died down.

"Good morning, everyone. First, I want to thank all of you who've been working under such intense pressure lately, especially thanks to those who interrupted their vacations to pitch in. We've been through a lot and need time to process everything. Many of us worked closely with Jan, and I'm sure some of you are questioning why we didn't see the signs of his struggles sooner. It's crucial to seek help if you need it; we've arranged for two excellent therapists to be available for debriefing sessions in the coming weeks." Erik paused, letting his words sink in before continuing. "On another note, we have some new faces joining us. Tomorrow, Ida Steen, our new chief forensic pathologist, will start. She's originally from Vidare Island and has been working in Iceland and the Netherlands. We'll also receive regular updates on the changes at the new lab, where there have been some procedural lapses." He gestured toward the man beside him.

"And I'm Grim Mattis, new to the team as a digital forensic technician, and I will work closely with you in certain cases."

Grim's calm gaze swept the room as he made eye contact with each person. Moa had to stifle a smile—the start of the meeting had the vibe of an AA gathering, and she half-expected everyone to chime in with, "Hi, Grim."

Erik continued, "We'll have a patrol stationed at the hotel in Nordby until thoroughly examined. Today, we'll continue our work around Jan's summer cottage. Before I wrap up, here is a quick reminder about the upcoming training days on nerve agents next week. There's new material to cover, and we're developing safer procedures, which you can read more about on the intranet. Also, take a few extra hours at the shooting range—as starting next year, we must pass the assessment test four times a year instead of two. Ylva?"

Ylva stood up and said, "Today's big news is the following: Sune Simonsen, the head of the narcotics division, has been arrested. He's been caught smuggling both weapons and drugs. The car part thefts I've been investigating also trace back to him, a key player in a criminal network.

He has started cooperating, and from what I've gathered, he gave orders to Jan, who passed them down the chain."

"Do we know who's at the top?" Erik asked.

"Not yet. But Jan's name has surfaced in several places. For instance, he was one of the investors in Green Air, a company planning to build more wind farms. That isn't illegal—Jan was a driven businessman—but somewhere along the line, things went awry. Based on what we've uncovered and recent events, it seems likely that he was struggling with a personality disorder. Ingrid overheard him talking to himself in different voices and dialects several times. I'll be questioning her, but it doesn't appear she was involved. Jan probably orchestrated Bernd's death. Analysis confirms that the feathers covering the body match those from the pillows and duvets at Jan's hotel."

Ylva spread two papers and continued, "These maps, found on a USB drive, were fantasies Jan used to lure investors. He called the project 'Major Tom' and used the alias 'Ziggy' in various media. The trail leads to businessmen from Saudi Arabia eager to invest in green energy production. Many new projects also receive EU support, and investing in European countries makes it easy to obtain an EU passport legally. With Jan's extensive contacts, it wasn't hard for him to sell the dream of a new life on the Friland Islands."

Ylva paused, scanning the room as she gauged her colleagues' reactions.

"It got out of his control—he couldn't separate reality from fantasy," Erik added, his bloodshot eyes betraying his sleepless nights. "But why did he kill Bernd Jung?"

"Success can easily cloud judgment," Ylva replied. "The most logical explanation is that Jan saw Bernd as a threat to his environmental ideals—Bernd was an obstacle to new developments that could harm the environment. When we found his phone, most of the data was wiped out, but we retrieved critical information from the telecom operator. There was a message on Bernd's phone to Rasmus: 'I'll tell you everything when we meet. I've got the proof.' That message was sent on the Friday before Bernd disappeared. On his Viber account, a message to Tim was found concerning a meeting. Tim has since been released, and no evidence links him to the crime. Before leaving, Tim gave us a warning. Let me quote his words."

Ylva picked up a piece of paper and read aloud, "The Friland Islands are turning into a playground for capitalists."

"There might be some truth to that," Grim interjected, drawing nods of agreement from around the room.

"But wasn't Bernd's phone found in Rasmus's apartment?" Moa asked, her voice cutting through the tension.

"It didn't take long for Jan to place it there on Tuesday after their meeting at the lighthouse," Ylva explained. "Rasmus was investigating a corruption case within the municipality that often led to shady building permits. Amid this, Tim Klein, the receptionist at Jan's hotel, became involved. He had uncovered Jan's schemes by overhearing too much. Tim opposed the wind farms and had arranged a meeting with Bernd. He was planning a protest, had already applied for a permit with the municipality, and had even started another Facebook group."

"Did the permit check out?" Erik asked, his interest piqued.

"Not only that. Henning, Jan's father, was the municipal manager and was heavily involved in stopping future developments in the area. Yet, Green Air still secured a permit. But I won't delve into politics."

Piece by piece, the puzzle began to come together. Ylva added, "It turns out that Jan had a drug addiction. I believe you found drugs in the bathroom cabinets yesterday?"

"Yes," Erik confirmed. "We found everything from lighter drugs to hard substances. Unfortunately, he hid it well and still did his job."

"So far, all signs point to Jan as the one who broke into the zoo in search of money. A woman contacted us yesterday. She had arranged to meet Rasmus via Tinder—they were supposed to have coffee on Tuesday afternoon instead of the evening because she couldn't find a babysitter. She's Finnish and was vacationing in Nordby with her daughter. Rasmus had told her he had a meeting with a colleague on Tuesday morning and was looking forward to the coffee date."

"Jan. At the lighthouse," Erik murmured, the pieces clicking into place.

Goosebumps prickled Moa's skin. Despite everything she had witnessed, she should have been desensitized by now. But death was creeping closer to her circle of colleagues.

"We suspected early on that someone had thrown Rasmus over the railing," Erik continued. "And now we're waiting for the DNA analysis on the remains found in the well on Jan's property. I guess that it's his ex-girlfriend. I believe Jan must have called her, asked her to get off the bus, and then picked her up."

"You found other things in Jan's cottage, right?" Ylva asked, turning to Moa.

"We found fifteen small birds in the freezer. They were an endangered species. The birds have been sent to the veterinary medical center for tests."

* * *

"For those interested, there's fresh coffee available. We've got a new machine, and you can grind your beans. Looks like they're pulling out all the stops to keep us happy," Erik said as the meeting wrapped up.

The room filled with light laughter and smiles as people began to stand up. Moa gathered her papers and followed the others. Grim quickly caught her attention, offering a handshake and showing genuine interest in getting to know his new colleagues.

"I wonder if we can order custom work clothes for you," Erik said, and everyone laughed.

Grim's bulging biceps immediately sparked a conversation about exercise and plans to get in shape.

But it's tough finding time. The kids. I used to work out.

Moa sipped her freshly ground coffee, which didn't taste significantly different from regular brewed coffee, letting the small talk temporarily overshadow the latest events. Her body and soul needed something beautiful to hold on to. Fredrik awaited her at the hotel, and she would go there, rest, and confide in him. It was time to open up and trust again, something she had avoided for years. Then, there was the trip to Greece, and she made a mental note to call her brother as soon as possible.

Ylva finished her coffee and joked with Erik that she should visit the forensic department more often.

Moa opened the door to her office, set down the stack of papers, and reached for her jacket. Although exhausted, she had made a difference, and the long hours were worth it. The victims had spoken, and she had listened.

EPILOGUE

The sky above Nordby was cloaked in a pink twilight as the sea calmly awaited the arrival of the night.

Moa sat on the beach with Fredrik. He picked up some small stones and held them in his hand.

"Look, a black sun," Moa said, pointing to the swarm of birds undulating the sky.

"A black sun?"

"That's what it's called. Starlings create this phenomenon before they settle for the night."

"There are many," he said, tossing a small stone.

"Around half a million."

She leaned her head against his shoulder.

"Moa, there are some things I want to tell you."

He turned toward her.

"Me too."

"Here," he said, placing the small stones in her hand. "Toss the first one. We've got plenty of time."

THE BETRAYED
The Friland Murders Book 2

A boat slows off the Friland Islands in the North Sea. The transponder goes dark as a man drifts to sleep in his car on deck. A hand signals the all-clear, and metal meets water. During a routine training dive near the oil platform, divers stumble upon a chilling discovery: a body strapped in a Ferrari at a depth of twenty-five meters. Forensic technician Moa Bakke and her team are called to the scene as newly appointed detective inspector Fredrik Dal eagerly begins his first day on the job.

The once-peaceful North Sea community gets caught in a chilling crime wave, shaking it to its core. As the investigation deepens, friendships fracture, loyalties are tested, and it becomes clear—everything has a price, even life itself.

Get your copy of *The Betrayed*, which is available on Amazon.

A NOTE FROM THE AUTHOR

I hope you enjoyed this book and felt immersed in the Nordic Noir experience. I aim to create a brief escape from the everyday world and knowing that my stories resonate with you means everything to me.

As a Scandinavian author, reaching a broader audience can be challenging, so your support makes a difference. Your engagement as a reader is what inspires me to keep writing.

I'd love to hear your thoughts! If you enjoyed the book, please consider leaving a review or recommending it to fellow readers. Your feedback helps me continue crafting stories you'll enjoy. Thank you for being such a loyal reader.

Victoria
vmlarsson.com

ABOUT THE AUTHOR

VM Larsson, a Swedish author, is fascinated by how life shapes us into who we are, and she embraces the challenge of capturing the complexities of human nature in her writing.

To perfect her craft, she immerses herself in textbooks and preliminary investigation reports while staying updated on the latest real-life drama in the news. Accurately portraying police procedures is essential for believability but must also serve the story.

When she is not writing, you'll likely find her strolling along deserted beaches, where the solitude sparks her imagination—perfect for dreaming up tales of serial killers and the heroes who bring them to justice.

Printed in Great Britain
by Amazon